To Tilly Jul

from

Thelgrawall.

RING 31265

RING 31265

by

F. M. GRAVATT

VICTORY PRESS
LONDON and EASTBOURNE

Printed in Great Britain for
VICTORY PRESS (Evangelical Publishers Ltd.),
Lottbridge Drove, Eastbourne, Sussex,
by Richard Clay (The Chaucer Press), Ltd.,
Bungay, Suffolk.

CHAPTER ONE

THE HOUSE IN LEWIS ROAD

Ross kept close to the tree, not wanting either Peter or Carol to catch sight of him. Below, obscured by the long grass, were his satchel and raincoat; but spring was not far enough advanced to provide for him any such green cover in the tree, whose branches spread dark and bare against the March sky.

He watched his brother and sister with their bikes—seventeen year old Peter with his cap set at a rakish angle on his thick straw-coloured hair, fourteen year old Carol, her straight blonde hair framing her thin face. Only last year Carol had been climbing trees with him, swimming, fishing, escaping to the sweet shop when they were in funds; now she considered his twelve years beneath her notice; now both she and Peter were like strangers who acted as though they had never been his age. They would cycle the two miles to Simms Grammar School, talking and laughing in their new understanding, in which he had no share.

Once they had gone, Ross relaxed. He had twenty minutes. They always left at half past eight, and it took him only five minutes to run up Lewis Road, over the High Street to his own secondary school.

"Morning, Mrs. Rich."

Ross started at the sound of Mrs. Hammond's voice hailing his mother from next door. Though they were hidden from his view by the part of their house that was built out into the garden, he could picture Mrs. Hammond peering over the fence to make sure everything in number thirty-two was in order.

From the tree at the end of the garden Ross could survey the backs of the houses in Lewis Road, with their grimy yellow bricks and grey slate roofs, their oblong sash windows and their untidy fences. But thirty and thirty-two had always been special. It was as though the builders had started each end of the road, then discovered when they came to the turn of the road that they were left with a spare piece of land, which they then divided between the two houses at the end of each terrace.

Ross turned from the houses on his left to what was happening beyond the other fence. Gone were the houses similar to his own, wiped out by the bulldozers. Instead, three blocks of flats rose grey and angular against the sky. It had been fun watching the mechanical digger, the crane, the concrete mixer; but now that exciting part was over. By the autumn the flats would be finished and the family would move in while the rest of Lewis Road was demolished. Peter and Carol were pleased at the idea, but Ross realised that more than ever he wanted this odd-shaped garden that had been his territory for so long as he could remember. From his high perch he looked down at their garden. He knew every bit of it—the tool shed with its woody smell, where he and Jeff Sampson spent hours and hours; the stumpy laurel tree where blackbirds nested every year, the lime tree in the corner where the owl would stay solitary before flying off into the night, the rubbish dump where the hedgehog had disappeared last autumn. It was like a map in his mind, a picture map, crowded with all the things that had ever happened there, as well as the things he planned. Now it was threatened.

Behind the back gardens was an approach road where the dustcarts lumbered along, just missing the fences; and on the other side of that was the park, a stretch of smooth grass broken by flower beds. Beyond was the dark barrier of Simms Wood, where he and Jeff could spend Saturdays and holidays undisturbed.

Ross looked anxiously at his watch. Five more minutes—the half exciting, half frightening time when he prolonged his stay in the garden, at the risk of being late for school, daring himself to steal another few moments' pleasure. Knowing he was at the limit, Ross scrambled down from the tree, picked up his raincoat and satchel, and slipped out into Lewis Road.

As he came in sight of the school he could distinguish Jeff peering round the gate.

"Rossy," yelled Jeff beckoning wildly.

Ross pushed in beside him and they caught up with the line of boys.

Mr. Forbes grunted, eyeing Ross. "Just in time."

Ross, too breathless to reply, followed Jeff into school.

CHAPTER TWO

SOUNDS IN THE NIGHT

His meal over, Ross stared out of the window that overlooked the garden at the back of the house. Since in a few months everything would be at the mercy of the builders, Mr. Rich had left things to go their own way; and though this meant Ross could do much as he pleased in the garden, it was an unwelcome reminder that soon there would be no private domain of his own.

Peter was arguing about politics, while Carol tried to look grown up. Bored with their talk, Ross listened to the rising wind, watching the bare branches whipped by its force. He noticed it was growing darker; perhaps it was going to rain.

"Put the light on, Carol, will you," said Mrs. Rich.

"Ross has finished; why can't he?" Carol wriggled her shoulders in the queer way she did these days.

"Carol!" reproved Mrs. Rich; but Ross sprang up quickly, switched on the light and escaped up the stairs.

Here it was even darker. He passed his parents' room, Peter's den, and the small room on the left that was Carol's, then made his way up the extra flight of stairs to the two attic rooms with sloping ceilings, which seemed as though they had been thrust into the roof. The one on the right was filled with lumber, oddments of wall-paper, a broken chair or two, picture frames. The other room was his. Ross switched on the electric fire, watching the brightness redden across the whole bar, then clambered onto the narrow bed which was placed along the wall on the left. Kneeling, he leant his elbows on the sill of the small window. From here he could view their extra bit of garden, and part of the flats on the other side. Almost out of his view, at the entrance to Lewis Road was the contractor's office, a sort of caravan affair, where the foreman made cups of tea, looked at plans, and interviewed the men. Through the window on the other wall one could see Simms Wood.

There was a sudden fierce downpour of rain, lashed against the window by the wind, blotting out the new building. Ross tugged at the curtains then turned on the light. On one side of the fire was a chest of drawers, on the other a cupboard which held all his belongings. A square of royal blue carpet was in the centre of the floor, while an oblong table with a wooden chair each end was in front of the other window. Ross took out the two new library books, fingering their shiny covers. Below, Peter's record-player started up; and Ross remembered that tonight he wanted to watch television. Forgetting the light and the fire, he raced downstairs.

Roused from sleep, Ross turned on his back, pulled the clothes closer about his shoulders and prepared to sink back into his pleasant dreams. The window frame rattled in the window. Ross opened his eyes, and though everything was in darkness he could see the curtains billowing out a little into the room, their flimsy material blown by the draught from the ill-fitting window. From the comfort of his bed, he watched their antics for a moment, safe from the chill wind that wrestled with them, then once more closed his eyes, enjoying the exciting sound of the wind. It was as he was drifting back into sleep that he heard the strange, disturbing call of the owl. Immediately he pushed back the bedclothes and knelt up at the small window, holding back the curtains so that he could peer into the night. The air was cold on his face. Outside in the garden it appeared lighter than in his room. One moment there were shadowy patterns on the grass, dancing replicas of the wind-blown branches; the next, as the moving clouds obscured the moon, the shadows were gone.

Ross waited, knowing the owl must be out of Simms Wood, or he would not have heard it so clearly. Patiently he watched the lime tree where at other times the owl had settled. Once more the clouds drifted on, leaving the pale moonlight to transform the scene, and in the new light Ross made out the dark shape of the owl. He could have missed it so easily, mistaken it for a bulge on that high branch. How small it looked, motionless, aloft in the tree. Now nothing mattered but keeping watch till the time came for it to make off in search of food, its wings spread in the darkness. The two watchers kept quite still, waiting.

A sudden sharp sound, like crashing tiles or breaking glass, disturbed their vigil, and the owl, warned by the alien noise, flew soundlessly into the night. Distracted by the commotion, Ross had taken his eyes off the owl, missing the very thing for which he had been waiting.

"Blow," he muttered, then began to wonder what it was beyond the lime tree that had startled both the owl and himself. He slipped his now chilly feet under the clothes, the picture of the owl still vivid in his mind, when he heard the stairs creak. The next moment a door opened, and Ross was alert, listening.

It was Peter, late again, and Dad was having something to say. Curious, Ross crept out of bed and opened his door quietly, then peered over the banister to the landing below. Though he could not see either of them, he could hear his father talking to Peter. Then the dim landing light was switched off, the doors closed, and everything was dark and silent once more. Ross shivered as he stole back to his own room, elated that no one else knew what he had heard that night—Peter and his father, the crash, and the call of the owl. There was something about creatures that moved at night which he couldn't describe. In the morning he'd enter it in his diary, about the owl; not about Pete—that wasn't anything special.

For a while Ross listened to the wind, thinking of the owl hunting the long night through and then before the first light hiding itself safely in Simms Wood.

At breakfast the next morning Peter was moody

and silent. He had been late down, so whatever it
was that Dad had threatened to have out with him
was still to come. Ross, however, felt jubilant, the
excitement of the night still with him, and the prospect of relaying it to Jeff added interest to the day.

"Can I go now, Mum?" He pushed back his
plate.

"You don't have to ask about everything," said
Peter scornfully.

Ross had half a mind to repeat part of what he'd
overheard last night, but it could wait. Pete was in
a rotten temper.

"You're much too early." Mrs. Rich eyed Ross.

"It's O.K.," he answered lightly, then went into
the hall for his cap and raincoat. Picking up his
satchel, he went out of the front door, then back
into the garden, going along by the side fence until
he came to the lime tree. He calculated just where
the owl had stayed last night, then considered the
sound that had driven it back to its own haunts. It
could have been something on the building site, or
it could have been on the pathway behind the
houses in Lewis Road. Dropping his satchel at the
foot of the lime tree, Ross followed the back fence
until he reached the gate; then, lifting the latch
carefully, not wanting to attract any attention from
the house, he went out onto the path and walked
slowly in the direction of the lime tree, looking for
anything that might have caused the sound in the
night. But there was nothing, not even when he
went some distance beyond the tree, only muddy
ruts and tufts of grass. The back fences of the
houses already demolished were in a rickety con-

dition, but he could see little by peering through the cracks. He made his way back to his own garden, intending to view the ground next door. By placing one foot on the cross beam of the fence and the other on the trunk of the tree, and using his hands and feet carefully, he managed to get onto the top of the fence without much effort. The wooden palings were none too stout, but, by holding onto the tree and leaning his weight against it, Ross could balance on the top of the fence and survey the scene below, and at the same time remain hidden from his own family. The actual flats were some distance away, and between was a variety of discarded material.

Ross kept still and hidden as he heard Peter and Carol with their bikes. Peter was having a lot to say now, though he had been so dumb at breakfast. When they were gone Ross turned his attention once more to the building site. His legs ached from keeping them in the same position for so long. He shifted his right foot to rest it on the top of another paling. Suddenly the wood gave beneath his weight; he clutched wildly at the tree, but it was too late. Ross fell heavily on the other side of the fence.

B

CHAPTER THREE

TRESPASSER

When Ross first opened his eyes, he could not re-
collect where he was; then as he saw the branches
of the lime tree spreading high above him, he remembered what had happened.

There was a sharp pain across his forehead, and
a rushing noise in his ears. For a moment he was
frightened lest he was badly hurt and unable to
move, but as he found his legs responded to his
efforts his fears subsided. He sat up, and felt his
forehead, touching it carefully. By his side was the
piece of crazy paving, a remnant of the old garden,
with which his head had collided, stunning him.
The drumming in his ears lessened, but his head
swam when he bent down to look at his watch. He
blinked, trying to make out the figures. Quarter
to nine—or had it stopped? It seemed so long ago
that he was holding onto the lime tree. Fortunately
he had fallen on his right side or the watch might
have been smashed.

He realised that the builders would be round
so he crouched against the fence, half-hidden by a
tufty lavender bush, hoping that no one would spot
him. All that mattered now was to get out without
endless questions and in time for school.

Along the Lewis Road side of the building site, a

temporary fence had been erected from remnants of the old front fences and ugly hoardings. A little way along were two barrier gates. These were open, and a lorry was backed onto the site, half-hiding the foreman's office. There was little chance of getting out that way without being seen. For a moment he stared miserably at the truck, its tail-board down, and a piece of rag tied onto the pro-truding load. A man came from the front of the lorry and Ross ducked. The only thing was to get over or through the other fence.

He closed his eyes for a moment, wishing that his head didn't hurt so much; then he got up and steadied himself against the fence. His hand was against the very piece of wood that had sent him off his balance. He could put his hand through and touch the trunk of the lime tree. Then he saw the narrow gap in the back fence. By pushing another paling to one side, he wriggled through without much difficulty. In the relief of being safe he forgot the blow on his head, but by the time he had reached the High Street he was once more aware of the pain. The skin was broken and blood was trickling onto his eyebrow. It was only when he went through the school gate that he remembered that his satchel was still in the garden.

Jeff had almost given him up, but from the end of the file of boys he was still anxiously waiting for Ross. He couldn't make it out that today, when Ross was later than usual, he was in no hurry to join the others. Then he saw the fast-swelling lump on Ross's forehead.

"What you done?" he exclaimed.

"Late again." Mr. Forbes had not failed to note Ross's arrival; then he, too, saw the damaged head. "What have you been up to?"

Ross tried to smile, but it didn't work. "I—I slipped, sir."

"And hit your head against the pavement, I suppose, by the looks of it." Mr. Forbes was bending over Ross. "Not surprised; look at your shoes, not done up. If you go around with dangling shoe-laces you must expect a knock or two."

"Yes, sir," said Ross meekly, relieved that he hadn't had to explain.

"Shall I take him to the First Aid Room, sir?" offered Jeff hopefully. He knew Ross hadn't just tripped over his shoe-laces, and he was curious.

"All right; but don't make a holiday of it."

For the rest of the morning, Ross sat listlessly at his desk. His head ached, but more worrying was the fact that he had kidded Mr. Forbes. Yet this did not stop him from scheming to do the same at home.

When Ross came by at midday, the gates onto the building site were closed, but his one thought was to retrieve his satchel before he went indoors.

He went slowly into the kitchen, where he and his mother always had lunch.

"Oh, Ross, who's been——" Her voice was full of concern. "You haven't been fighting?"

"No; it's O.K., Mum."

"Then what happened?"

"I was climbing——"

Mrs. Rich knew all too well his craze for climb-

ing trees. It must have been the chestnut trees outside the playground again. Last summer he had
ripped a shirt, scrambling down.

"Ross, I wish you'd be more careful. It's only
just missed your eye. Did you fall?"

"Mm." Ross let her go on, aware that he was
deceiving her, and knowing from experience that
this way she would probably forget to ask any more
questions.

"Perhaps you'd better stay home."

"I'm O.K. Mrs. Rayner did it up; she said it 'ud
be all right." All the same, he reckoned he wouldn't
go this afternoon; he did feel rather odd.

"Was Jeff climbing, too?"

"No, he was in the playground."

"That's good. You'd better eat some dinner."

Ross made a valiant effort to deal with the plate
of stew.

"You aren't going this afternoon," Mrs. Rich
said firmly.

Ross pushed the plate aside, then listened for the
sound of Jeff racing down the path at the side of
the house, half afraid of his letting out the truth of
what had really happened.

CHAPTER FOUR

UNWELCOME CALLER

By the time the rest of the family came home, Ross had revived, and if it hadn't been for the niggling fear of discovery he would have enjoyed his father's concern and Carol's surprise. Even Peter forgot to be stand-offish and joked with him about tackling Mount Everest one day. He could have been quite a hero, but he knew he was cheating them all.

So they finished the evening meal. As Mrs. Rich looked round at the empty plates, there was a ring at the front door.

"I'll go." Ross pushed back his chair, anxious to avoid any further attention. Somehow, one story had led to another, and the simple escapade of looking over his own garden fence had developed into something quite different. If only he hadn't begun it!

The front door was stiff; and, before he managed to open it, Ross was aware that he had left the dining-room door open and that the others were listening.

"Oh," said Ross looking up at the policeman.

"My! you look as though you'd been in the wars," he said jovially.

"It's nothing," mumbled Ross, desperately wanting to escape.

"Perhaps I could have a word—ah, good evening, madam."

Mrs. Rich came forward, and Ross was trapped between the two of them.

"We were wondering if you might be able to help us with some enquiries."

"Why yes, of course; come in, will you." She was a little flustered. "I'll fetch my husband." But having heard the stranger's voice, the family had already come into the hall. The policeman entered and Ross closed the door, glad to shelter behind his bulky form. Any other time he would have hung around out of sheer curiosity; now he longed to escape. He just didn't want to risk being asked how he came by the blow on his head.

The red lamp-shade shed a strange, fiery glow on the six figures gathered in the hall. Mr. Rich smoothed back his hair, then thrust his hands in his pockets, prepared to enjoy the situation. "Well, we're all here; what can we do to help you?"

"It's about the building site. You being next door, we thought you might have heard or seen something that would be of assistance in our enquiries." Now Ross was terrified. Not that the policeman could accuse him of anything, but the very mention of the building site was an uncomfortable reminder of his deception.

"What's the problem?" Mr. Rich was facing the policeman, while Mrs. Rich stood on his left by the stairs. Peter and Carol were against the wall on their father's right, so that Ross sheltered by the policeman's form was hidden from them all.

"Appears to be a bit of a strange affair; some

valuable tools missing and a certain amount of interference."

"I see," said Mr. Rich slowly. "Any clues?"

"Well——" The policeman rubbed his chin thoughtfully. "Nothing definite. We want to establish the time of the theft so that we can rule out certain individuals. Now, if you heard or saw anything suspicious last night, this could give us a lead."

"I did." It was out before Ross realised what he had done.

All eyes were on him now.

"And when was this?" The policeman moved to one side, so that Ross was confronted with all of them.

"Last night."

"About what time?"

"I—I don't know."

"Roughly, then."

"Well, I was watching the owl—it was in the lime tree; I can see it from the window above my bed."

"Bird-watching, eh," said the policeman, and he gave a condescending smile, the sort of smile that says 'My, you're quite a little fellow, aren't you.' "That how you managed the tumble?"

"No, that was this morning. The owl wouldn't be around then."

Peter sniggered and Ross got angrier.

"I'd been to sleep and it woke me up. I know it settles in the lime tree in the corner against the fence, so I looked out to see if it was there."

"What time d'you go to bed?" asked the policeman.

"Between half past eight and nine," said Mrs. Rich, wondering what Ross was going to say next.

"And what else did you hear beside this owl. An owl isn't exactly evidence—we can't question an owl, can we?"

"No." Ross tightened his lips. Why did people have to say silly things as though he didn't understand? "It was another sound like something being smashed."

"Couldn't have been the owl," mocked Peter.

"I know an owl if you don't. Anyway, this sound was close and it startled the owl and it flew off."

"Well, we might have something here. But you didn't see anything?"

"It was dark. I mean you could only make things out, when the clouds weren't over the moon."

Peter was leaning against the wall, looking down at his feet, half smiling.

"But you can't tell me the time?" continued the policeman.

Peter half turned to Carol, and Ross sensed there was some secret joke they shared. He was mad with them; they treated him like no one, as if he didn't matter, as if the things he did weren't important.

"Yes, I can," answered Ross sullenly.

"I thought just now you couldn't," said Peter lazily.

"Well, it was just before you came in."

There was a strained silence, and Ross wished desperately that he could recall the words, for now

the policeman's attention was focused on Peter.
Too late, Ross realised that Peter might have some
reason for belittling his evidence. He glanced at
his mother and saw her troubled look.

"And what time would that be?"

For a moment Peter hesitated.

"You sure you heard Pete, Ross?" asked Mr.
Rich.

"Yes, Dad."

"We don't want to give a wrong time." Mr. Rich
appeared calm but Ross knew he was angry.

"No, Dad."

"Well, what makes you so sure you heard Peter
come in? As far as I know he didn't utter a word."

"I know."

"Well?"

"But you did, Dad."

"Oh?"

It was still a question, and it nettled Ross. "You
said freedom was one thing, but this was carrying
things——"

"O.K., O.K. It was Peter you heard coming upstairs."

"And the time?" pursued the policeman.

"About a quarter to twelve," answered Mr. Rich
testily.

"Quarter to twelve. I see. Now, Peter, did you
observe anything unusual on your way home?"

"No, nothing unusual."

"Which way did you come home?"

For a moment Peter hesitated. "The road at the
back of the houses."

"So you came in through the back gate."

Again Peter hesitated. "No, actually I didn't; the gate was locked when I tried it."

"Oh, so you had to walk right to the other end, to the High Street, behind the building site, and then back again down Lewis Road in front of the site. That means you would have had a very good chance of hearing anything that was going on."

"I suppose I would."

"But in actual fact you heard nothing at all. On your own, were you?"

"No, I was with a friend."

"Perhaps your friend heard or observed something. It might be worth trying."

Peter was silent, and now the policeman was watching him closely. "Not afraid your information doesn't tally with his, by any chance?"

"No, I just don't tell on my friends. I shall let him know what's happened, and then it's up to him." Peter was angry.

"Just thought it would be useful to have his comments."

Peter laughed. "On one of Ross's noises in the night? I wouldn't spend any time on them."

"Well, I'll say goodnight. Goodnight, madam."

Ross opened the door, and they watched the policeman walking slowly to the iron gate. Then, when the door was closed, the family was alone. Peter pushed past Ross up to his own room, and the next moment they heard his record-player going.

"Well, you're a rotten tell-tale," accused Carol, tossing her head.

Ross couldn't think of any answer, and what if

they knew he had been fooling them?

"That's not quite fair, Carol," said Mr. Rich. "Peter had no right to poke fun at things that are of interest to other people. He egged Ross on. Don't think I'm standing up for you, Ross; it would have been a sight better for all of us if, instead of hiding everything you do, you were reasonably open."

Mrs. Rich sighed, aware that there was still a great deal that Ross was concealing.

"He's always on at me," complained Ross.

"Well, it seems to have been a bad day all round. How about you, Carol? You got anything cheerful to report?"

"Not much." She smiled, and things were easier.

Ross went upstairs slowly. On the dark landing he listened to the vibrating music, then made his way to his own room. He knelt up at the window and stared out at the lime tree in the growing dusk. There was a storm coming; the wind that had dropped during the day had renewed its force, and had the trees at its mercy. Ross could not shake off the sense of shame that he had betrayed Peter. Then he began to wonder about his brother. Was he, too, hiding something?

CHAPTER FIVE

31265

Breakfast was a silent and uncomfortable meal, and at the first opportunity Ross escaped from the company of Peter and Carol. In the hall he pushed his plimsolls into his satchel, then reached for his raincoat.

Mrs. Rich came out. "You can't call for Jeff yet; you know Mrs. S doesn't like you too early."

Ross didn't look up. "I'm not going yet; I want to see if the shed's all right after that rain."

"Oh, all right." Mrs. Rich went into the kitchen. Peter and Carol came into the hall but they ignored Ross. He still felt the weight of all that had happened the previous evening. He unlocked the kitchen door and went out. After the storm everything was saturated, each tall blade of grass was set with drops of rain, the earth was sodden, the bark of the trees dark and damp. Ross walked down the garden, then along by the back fence until he was out of view of the kitchen window. Stopping at the laurel tree with its thick rain-washed leaves and its untidy shape, he peered into the branches to see what progress if any the blackbird had made with her nest. It was chilly here, and the drips of rain from one leaf to another made the only sound. He stooped to avoid a branch, when something on the ground attracted his notice. For a moment he would not touch it, but remained staring at the lifeless blackbird whose feathers were heavy with rain. Then he caught sight of the whitish aluminium ring on its leg. Forgetting about school and Peter, Ross let his satchel drop to the ground, and picked up the bird that had obviously met with disaster in last night's storm. It was strange holding the stiff form. Once in the shed Ross carefully removed the ring and read the message out loud.

Inform British Museum, S.W.7. 31265R. Holding the dead blackbird he had felt angry, but the small ring in the palm of his hand now filled Ross with excitement; something about the number so clearly indicated on the metal set him thinking. Not wanting to go indoors again he placed the ring carefully in a wooden box that held some oddments of pencils and card, planning what he and Jeff would do about it. All the way up to school the number kept going through his mind, 31265R.

"You sure it's all right for you to come down here at lunch time?" Mrs. Rich asked as Jeff came into the kitchen; but he only looked innocent, his slanting blue eyes half closed by the broad grin that spread over his face. You couldn't help noticing Jeff, and, whereas he was slow and deliberate in his movements, when it came to seeing a joke Jeff was always first.

Now the two boys escaped into the garden, and together they examined the minute circle of metal. Jeff's fingers trembled as he picked it up. Ross often wondered why Jeff's fingers shook whenever he picked things up, small things, as though because his hands were large they couldn't cope with little things.

"Tell you what," said Jeff.

Ross looked up.

Jeff laughed. "You better have a burial service."

"Oh, I'll—oh, O.K." Intent on the ring he had almost forgotten the blackbird.

"We going to write?" queried Jeff.

"You bet." But Ross knew Jeff would never manage the letter. It was the same with an essay at school; he could never come up to the point of deciding how to begin.

"Then they'll tell you where he——"

"She," corrected Ross; "you can tell by the colour, silly."

Jeff rubbed his head, grinning. His eyes were bright; it was here in the freedom of Ross's garden, or in Simms Wood, that he enjoyed himself. "What you going to put?"

"Dunno, really."

"Ask your mum," advised Jeff. Adults never seemed to suffer from the inability to start a letter.

Ross, too, was relieved that he need not make the effort. Writing letters was a trial. He frowned. A letter meant an answer, and he didn't want Peter and Carol to know anything. Once more the previous evening's affair came back to his mind. For a while he had escaped it; now it was disturbing him.

"O.K., we'll ask my mum." He closed the shed door behind them.

"Old Forbes 'ud be surprised," remarked Jeff. They were both aware that they were not in their teacher's good books, both aware, too, that they rarely did anything at school to merit any praise.

"Mum," called Ross. They came into the kitchen, leaving a trail of muddy footprints. "Mum, we've got a letter to write."

"For school—then you'll have to do it yourselves."

"Course not for school," said Jeff.

"Oh." Mrs. Rich was interested to know what could have stirred them to want to write a letter.

Ross began to explain the situation while his mother continued washing up, and he held out the small ring for her to see.

"I think its a good idea. Fetch your biro; and Jeff, you'll find some paper and envelopes in the dresser drawer there."

"Mum." Ross was fidgeting with his biro. "Me and Jeff, we want it to be——"

Mrs. Rich looked at Ross, wondering why nowadays he kept so many things to himself. "You want it to be private."

"Yes, just me and Ross," grinned Jeff.

"Mum, suppose Pete——"

"Picks up your answer when it comes?"

"Mm."

"Well, what would Peter say if you wanted to know what was in one of his letters?"

Ross laughed nervously, aware that he was making a fuss. "He'd say, Mind your own business, you——"

"Well, I guess you could say the same to him. But you can't always keep things secret."

"I got the paper ready." Jeff was waiting.

"You'll want two envelopes, Jeff, one stamped and addressed to yourselves to put in with the letter." Mrs. Rich dried her hands then took two stamps from her purse. "Jeff, you can address one of the envelopes to Ross, while he writes the letter."

Jeff wrote slowly, Ross Rich, 32 Lewis Road, Hamstorth.

Mrs. Rich began to dictate to Ross.

"Dear Sir,
"Would you please let me have details of number 31265R. I would like to know where the bird was ringed and by whom. This blackbird was found in my garden, and I think it was killed by the storm last night.

"From Ross Rich."

Ross folded the letter carefully, inserting the envelope addressed to himself. If only he didn't have to wait too long! "I'm going to put the ring away." He ran upstairs.

"When d'you think we'll hear?" Jeff watched Mrs. Rich addressing the envelope to the British Museum.

"Depends how busy they are. Let's see, it's Wednesday today—you might hear on Monday."

Jeff picked up the letter. "Wish I'd found that bird."

"For goodness sake hurry or you'll be late for school." Mrs. Rich hustled Jeff out of the kitchen.

C

CHAPTER SIX

IN SIMMS WOOD

Jeff pushed his feet under the brown leaves that had covered the ground since the autumn. The faint rustling made by the movement of his feet broke in on the intense quiet of the wood. Ross trod more lightly, hardly disturbing the leaves, thrusting his cap into his raincoat pocket and feeling the coolness of Simms Wood through his hair. Always it was cooler here: in summer the trees shielded you from the sun, in winter they sheltered you from the wind, so that even now there was hardly enough breeze to lift the lank fair hair from his forehead. His slight form was in strange contrast to Jeff's more solid build, but to each the sense of freedom here lent excitement to their outing. The knowledge that lingering here after school would make them late home, and bring a reprimand, could not keep them away from Simms Wood. The smell of the dark earth, renewed years without end by the falling leaves, and heavy with recent rain, was something they could not describe. Now the transformation of spring had begun, the hazy green look of twigs, the warmer air.

"Saw one," whispered Jeff, halting in his progress, and nudging Ross. They stood still, watching the grey squirrel halfway up a tree trunk. It turned as if to reprimand them for intruding, its tail tawny brown at the edges.

Jeff was tense with the secrecy of Simms Wood. the unexpected things that happened here, the awareness that, however quiet it was, something was going on.

The afternoon sun was waning, yet in places it still tinged the fallen leaves with a little of the bronze they had had in the autumn. Ross knew it was time to be going back, and that brought the unpleasant thought of Peter—Peter and the policeman. And then, like one of the slanting rays of light that penetrated through the leafless trees, something came to him about Peter. That gate wasn't locked; he remembered quite clearly what he did the next morning—how his mother had cautioned him about going too early, and how he had immediately said he'd intended going to the shed to see that it was all right after the storm. Then he had unlocked the kitchen door leading to the garden; but when he reached the gate from the garden to the back road, that had needed no unlocking; the bolt was not shot, nor was the key turned. When Peter was asked if he had come in that way, he had to take a chance, and he had guessed wrongly. Then why, if Peter came home that way, why didn't he even try the gate?

"Say, Jeff!" Ross had already regaled his friend with the affair of the previous evening. The squirrel darted up the tree and was lost to view. Ross came close to Jeff. "I've just thought of something."

"What?"

"Our gate. It wasn't locked, so Pete could have come in that way."

"You sure?" Jeff disliked troublesome things, nevertheless there was something exciting about this affair.

"Course I'm sure. Tell you why. Because yesterday I remember going straight out into the roadway to see if someone had been messing around smashing milk bottles. And I remember the gate wasn't bolted."

"You mean Pete never tried to get in."

"S'right. He never tried it. He was making it up about——" Now the doubts were there. They both knew Peter got up to things, rags, demonstrations. Yet, for Ross, the knowledge of his brother's guilt seemed to make his own offence smaller, even nothing in comparison. The queer thing was that Peter made trouble for himself by the way he answered the policeman.

The two moved slowly between the trees, tracing their way back home. Another thought came to Ross, but this he kept to himself. Suppose Mum remembered that she hadn't bolted that gate, that after the dustman's visit the previous day she had forgotten to lock it. Then she would know Peter was lying. Would she do anything about it? And suppose by some equally small thing his parents knew about his deception. Simms Wood no longer drew him; he felt miserable and afraid. Where was Peter that night? For when the policeman had said, "So you went all the way up the back road to the High Street and then back again. You would have had a good chance of hearing anything that was going on", he had merely replied, "I suppose I would." He had never admitted coming all the way round. So where did he go? Was he on the building site?

CHAPTER SEVEN

THE REPLY

On Monday morning Ross lingered in the hall, hoping that the post would arrive before he was called in to breakfast, watching the front door with its dingy brown paint. Even so the sharp snap of the letter-box startled him. As he pounced on the one or two letters that fell on the door-mat, he saw Jeff's round handwriting. Thrusting the precious letter in his blazer pocket, he called out, "There's a letter for you, Dad."

At the table Peter and his father began arguing about cars. Any other time Ross would have interrupted them with his own opinions, but now his one thought was to get away and read his letter without the others wanting to know who had written to him.

"I've finished," he announced, after gulping down the remnants of hot tea.

"So what," commented Carol.

Mrs. Rich looked across at Ross. He grinned, which meant 'It has come on Monday', and made for the door.

Unfolding the typewritten paper in his own room, he began to read the letter out loud.

"Dear Mr. Rich,

"Thank you for the information you submitted, which will be of assistance in our work. Enclosed are the details for which you enquire."

Then there was a signature which looked like 'S. Marks', and at the top was a reference number.

But it was another flimsy blue paper inside the letter which intrigued him most—a printed slip with columns for different sorts of information. From this he learned that the blackbird had been ringed in the spring of last year by Mr. Alexander Wilson, at the Old Barn, Wicket Lane, Hamstorth. Plans began racing through his mind; plans for Jeff and himself to visit Wicket Lane. He pictured the Old Barn and Alexander Wilson. This morning he couldn't wait till school-time before he saw Jeff, so, carefully placing the letter in his inside pocket, he picked up his satchel and ran downstairs. As he took his raincoat from the peg, he could hear Peter still going on about Jaguars.

"Cheerio, Mum," called Ross, then slammed the front door behind him, and ran out into Lewis Road. When he reached the High Street, he turned left and slackened his pace. Sampson's bakery opened at eight o'clock; and between the rows of new bread, sugared doughnuts, and pastries in the window, Ross could see Jeff's mother busy serving. He slipped down the passage-way which led to the yard and the bakehouse. Here he was met by the strange and delicious smell of freshly baked bread, and by Mr. Sampson in a white overall, carrying a large, wooden tray of rolls. He was a tall thin man whose face was nearly as white as the floury rolls. His eyes were blue like Jeff's, but because of the baker's hat he wore it was impossible to see if his hair matched Jeff's for darkness.

"Hullo, you want Jeff?" he called, then proceeded on his way to the shop. Ross looked round, fascinated by the high, window-shaped door from which sacks of flour used to be unloaded, by the rickety wooden steps which led to Mr. Sampson's office, by the large, ill-fitting garage doors, and the cobbled yard. Yet even so it did not compare with the garden and the shed at Lewis Road, for here at Sampson's one might not explore, nor touch, nor know what was going on. Here it was 'Keep out of the way. Hands off.' Here they were always busy, always telling you what to do. Here you could never be on your own and just make plans. Sampson's was like forbidden territory.

Jeff appeared at the back door, with his satchel and raincoat.

"So long, son," said Mr. Sampson, recrossing the yard.

"So long, Dad," replied Jeff.

Ross gave one last look at the strange old place that soon was to share the fate of Lewis Road and be replaced by up-to-date buildings. "I got it," he declared excitedly, diving into his pocket.

Jeff grinned, hitching his satchel over his shoulder. "What's it say? Let's have a look." They bent closely over the blue paper.

"Look, it was ringed last spring," said Ross.

"Alexander Wilson," read Jeff, "The Old Barn, Wicket Lane. Then we can go there."

"Course we can."

"When we going?" Jeff was all for any expedition, any escape from the routine of school and the shop. "After school, eh?"

Ross was doubtful; it was quite a step to Wicket Lane, yet how could one wait? Nor was Jeff one to wait; and sometimes Saturdays for him were busy—since his parents were so busy, they often needed him to run errands.

"Let's go after school," Jeff insisted.

"O.K.," agreed Ross. "I've got the letter." He refolded it and replaced it in his pocket; then, lighthearted, the two of them went on their way to school.

CHAPTER EIGHT

THE OLD BARN

Hurrying along the path that skirted Simms Wood, the two at last emerged into Wicket Lane. On the left were red brick cottages with long front gardens bordered by hedges, while on the right were larger houses, each with its own vegetable patch or small orchard at the side.

"That's it." Jeff pointed at the five-bar gate that was pushed back against the hedge.

Ross read the faded letters, 'The Old Barn'.

The house was to the left; by its side was a stack of crates, an old bicycle and a ladder, while directly in front of Ross and Jeff was a stretch of uncultivated ground.

"Come on," urged Jeff, waiting for Ross to lead the way. Ross considered the house and its forbidding front door. It would be easier to walk round the back, the same way that it was easier to walk into Sampson's yard than to go into the shop. Now that they were here, they were half reluctant to enter the Old Barn. They trod warily, the place was so quiet. Then they saw him, looking over his gold-rimmed spectacles at an array of plants in the conservatory. From a safe distance they watched him, wondering if this could be Mr. Alexander Wilson.

Jeff nudged Ross. "Come on."

Ross still hesitated; he knew he would have to make the first move, and yet a great many of the things they did together he would never attempt without Jeff.

"O.K.," decided Ross, and at that moment the man looked up and saw the two boys staring at him.

They went towards him.

"Ah." He peered at them over his spectacles, as he opened the door of the conservatory. Ross could feel the warmth of the place, and there was that close, earthy smell, rather like Simms Wood.

"We came to see Mr. Wilson." Ross felt for the letter while the man pushed back his cloth cap and surveyed his visitors.

"Mr. Wilson, eh?"

"Yes please." Jeff was eager to take some part in the proceedings.

"Well, that's just what you're doing—seeing Mr. Wilson."

"Oh," said Ross, noting the slightly foreign accent. Mr. Wilson didn't look as old now that he was talking with them as when he was bending over the plants.

"You got it, Ross?" prompted Jeff.

"It's this letter," explained Ross.

"Letter, eh? Now, since you know my name, supposing you tell me yours."

"I'm Jeff—Jeff Sampson; and he's Ross Rich."

"Jeff and Ross." Mr. Wilson cocked his head to one side and considered them. "I think I have seen you at church—in the High Street—isn't that right?"

"Yes, we go there." Jeff was pleased Mr. Wilson remembered them.

"Now, this letter."

"It was this blackbird," began Ross. "I found a ringed blackbird. It was killed by the storm the other night, so me and Jeff wrote to the British Museum."

"And you want to know all about it." Mr. Wilson took the letter and scanned its contents, half talking to himself. "Yes, that's one of my blackbirds, beaten down by the storm." Then to Ross and Jeff, "Now we'll fetch my records."

They followed him into an outhouse whose window overlooked the patch of tall grass and weeds interspersed with stunted apple trees. Inside was a long, wooden bench, a chair, and in the far corner, in strange contrast to the old place, a modern steel filing cabinet. On the rough bench was an assortment of coloured cards and a pair of binoculars, while on a table the other side of the room was a large box, some brownish netting and a cage-like affair. Important-looking charts were displayed on the walls, some with graphs, some with series of coloured dots on maps. In a wooden frame was a certificate. Printed at the top was 'British Trust for Ornithology', then some smaller printing, and, in flowing handwriting, 'Alexander Wilenski'. Mr. Wilson smiled at their interest. "You like my place?"

Ross was intrigued by the queer lilt in his voice.

"That's my patch, too." He pointed to the scrubby orchard beyond. "They like it here; a great many of them come, a very great many—greenfinches, magpies. You see if you can spot any while I look at my records." He handed the binoculars to Ross, then went across to the filing cabinet.

Ross tried to focus the binoculars.

Mr. Wilson's voice came from the corner where the filing cabinet stood. "Now, about that blackbird; yes, it was last spring I ringed her, and I'm sorry she won't be there to see this spring."

Ross listened. Now he could see the furthest trees, the branches hardly showing any sign of spring.

Mr. Wilson came across to him. "You know, I'm concerned about that blackbird you found—31265R. You know, it matters to God, too, even with all the others that are left. Ever thought about that? He sees when they fall to the ground."

Ross re-adjusted the binoculars. He couldn't see that it made any difference about God caring, since the blackbird was dead anyway.

"Oh yes, there's quite a bit in the Bible about it, but"—here he raised the hand that held the slip of blue paper—"He minds about us a lot more, says we're much more valuable. Ever thought of that, you two? No, I don't suppose you have; been too busy."

Jeff rubbed his head. "Dunno, really."

"So you see," Mr. Wilson was now looking at a white card he had taken from the filing cabinet, "when you fell to the ground, He minded about that."

Ross started. He lowered the binoculars, and his hand went up to the bruise which still discoloured his forehead. How did Mr. Wilson know he'd fallen? It could have been a fight, or a ball; but of course he was only comparing. All the same, he had noticed that mark. Why did things keep reminding him?

Mr. Wilson bent over the bench and, taking up his biro, wrote something at the bottom of the card. "There now. Yes, I ringed her in the orchard there; it was a beautiful day."

"How d'you do it? I mean, how d'you catch them to ring them?" enquired Ross.

"I have several methods; you come one day and I'll explain to you. In your Easter holidays, soon. How about that?"

"You mean we can come again?" asked Jeff.

"That's what I mean."

"Aw, thanks."

"You like it here; you have no place like Ross?"

"He's got the bakery," interrupted Ross.

"Ah yes, Sampson's bakery. Very fine bread, Sampson's. Now, I think it is time you went home for your tea. Suppose you come on Saturday—that's not so long to wait as the holidays—in the afternoon."

There was a whistle from the house. "That will be my tea."

They said goodbye, turning at the gate to wave, then ran out into Wicket Lane, Ross still holding the blue paper that reported on 31265R.

CHAPTER NINE

THE PLOT THICKENS

Although they all hoped the uncomfortable affair of the policeman's visit was past and done with, there was only one thought in their minds when the door-bell rang. Everything was the same as on that other evening; the sky was darkening, while in the corner of the dining-room the artificial flames of the electric fire glowed orange and red.

This time Ross made no attempt to answer the door. Peter had one hand in his pocket, while the other was stretched across the table drumming with a fork. It was a favourite attitude of his. Now he ceased his fidgeting with the fork and, looking up, saw the sudden fear that showed in his brother's eyes. Carol, too, glared at Ross, blaming him for any trouble that Peter was in.

"Oh dear, I hope it's not——" Mrs. Rich rose to answer the door.

"Of course not," reassured Mr. Rich laughingly, pushing back his chair. He went across to the window, whistling softly, while all of them were listening for the voice in the hall.

Mrs. Rich returned, and they knew by her look who the caller was. "It's a few more questions, Peter."

"Ah! Evening, sir; sorry to bother you." The

policeman had followed Mrs. Rich, and was now surveying the family, and the remnants of the meal.

"Oh, no bother at all." Mr. Rich came forward. All the same, he was annoyed to find they were once more at the mercy of his questioning. Last time had been most unpleasant, with Peter's stubbornness about his friend. Carol, toying with the strands of her blonde hair, was half excited and half afraid. Peter had boasted about the way he had stood up to the policeman, and, although he had refused to tell her who had been with him on that night, she had a pretty good idea who it was. Stephen Yates. But she couldn't understand why Peter was so fussy about it.

"Will you have a cup of tea?" offered Mrs. Rich.

"Well, I wouldn't say no."

Peter smiled, a small, superior smile. It was just what he had expected the policeman to say. Mr. Rich frowned impatiently. Now they were in for a long session, the policeman with a cup of tea to hang out the whole affair. Carol was sent for another cup and saucer; then, as Mrs. Rich poured the tea, the policeman looked round at the three, who, it seemed to him, shared some secret. After helping himself to two spoonfuls of sugar, he addressed Peter:

"I was wondering if you had come to any decision—regarding your friend, that is." He stirred the tea slowly, keeping his eyes on Peter.

Peter picked up the fork, then released it. "I gave you my decision last week." His manner was curt, and Mrs. Rich moved her hands nervously, understanding Peter's loyalty to his friend, yet aware that his decision and his attitude only made him more suspect.

"Stalemate, then," observed the policeman.

"'Fraid so," said Peter. "I have mentioned it to my friend, so it's not up to me now. There's nothing more I can do." He was moving the fork to and fro, trying to appear casual.

"I don't know about that. If your friend wants to deprive you of an alibi, I wouldn't put much on his friendship."

"I don't tell on my friends," flashed Peter, "and I don't see why I need an alibi for coming home."

"Have it your own way, though there's other ways of finding out. Just at the moment you happen to be the only person, apart from this anonymous friend of yours, whom we know was in the vicinity of the building site between the time when things were in order and the time the trouble was reported."

"Surely there was the night watchman," objected Mr. Rich.

"That's another story."

Mr. Rich frowned at Peter. "Well, it seems that's all we can do for you, officer." He was hoping the policeman would take this as his dismissal. But the cup of tea was not yet touched; the policeman was in no hurry.

The whole time Ross had hardly moved; he sat there tense, wondering if the policeman had discovered anything about Peter.

"There's just one other little matter." The policeman raised his cup and sipped the hot tea, aware that his words had put them all on their

D

guard once more. He was convinced they knew
something, though the man and his wife seemed
straightforward enough. Ross waited, stealing a
glance at Peter.

"And what's that?" Mr. Rich prepared for
another bout of questions.

Slowly the policeman replaced the cup on the
saucer, then turned to the waiting family. "As you
will understand, we have been making enquiries in
the vicinity, owing to there having been an increase
in the number of these, er, attacks on property."
It was the same deliberate manner, keeping them in
suspense. "It's the small things, sir, that often help.
You never know where or when they're going to fit
in." It was as though he was warning Mr. Rich that
there was worse to follow. "I understand from these
enquiries that on the morning of Tuesday of last
week, at approximately nine o'clock, though the
lady in question wouldn't swear to the exact time,
the young man here was observed entering the
building site."

"He couldn't have." Carol was up in arms.

"And how do you make that out?" He was watching her carefully, calculating where she fitted into
the plot.

"Because we were together; we cycled to school,
and at nine o'clock we were in school; and even if
he'd dashed back after we got to school, he couldn't
have done it." She paused for breath. "So it wasn't
Peter."

For a moment the room was quiet; the policeman, who had refused to sit down, was raising himself slightly on his toes, then lowering himself onto

his heels, trying to size up this awkward trio. Ross glanced at Carol, Carol who was standing up for Peter.

"Of course, miss, I'm not denying you went to school together," and now his voice was more coaxing, "but I'm not aware that I accused Peter Rich of anything."

Ross dare not look at the policeman, but he could picture the smile, the sinister, sure smile of someone who has got you tied up and knows you can't escape.

"But——" faltered Carol, gaping at the policeman, angry that she had made a silly of herself for nothing.

"It was the other young man I was referring to." How confidently he came out with the fatal words, every one of them like a chill to Ross's heart.

"Oh!" exclaimed Carol, slowly realising the meaning of his words.

Ross could feel the colour rising to his face; his mouth was dry, and not for anything could he look up, even though he knew that by his very attitude he was admitting his guilt.

"Ross, you!" Peter was really mad.

"Quiet!" ordered Mr. Rich. "Is this true, Ross?"

"Yes, Dad." He felt alone and afraid, cut off from them all.

"But what were you doing?" Mrs. Rich was puzzled and dismayed.

"Why weren't you at school?"

Ross stole a glance at the policeman who had caught him out so cleverly. Part of him was angry at being trapped, part of him was relieved that no longer need he worry about anyone discovering Tuesday's misadventure. It all seemed so stupid now. Why had he told those lies?

"Well, young man, we're waiting." It was an order not to be disregarded.

"I was early," began Ross, his voice hardly audible, "so I climbed on the fence behind the lime tree."

"And why did you choose this particular spot overlooking the building site?"

"Well, it was——" How was he going to explain, and why should they believe him? "It was the owl——"

"Oh, the owl." Ross hated the way he said it.

"Crumbs, not that again," muttered Peter.

"Go on," said the policeman, but Ross sat there sullenly. They had no right to treat him like this, just because he was only twelve.

"Go on, Ross." Mr. Rich's voice was sharp.

"I told you before. When I saw the owl that night, when it was startled and flew off, I guessed the sound came from somewhere quite close behind him; so I reckoned if I could look over the fence, I might find out what had disturbed him."

"And did you find out?"

"There were some tiles; they were yellow, and some of them were broken. It could have been them, someone knocking their foot against them."

The policeman had his hand over his mouth, his biro cocked beneath his forefinger, considering Ross. "Mm. And then?"

"I was standing on the top of the fence, holding

onto the tree, with one hand, so that I didn't over-balance; but the paling slipped sideways beneath my foot, and I fell over the other side."

"So you say you fell over there. But you could have been meaning to climb over there." He was watching Ross.

"If I'd climbed over there properly, I wouldn't have crashed on that bit of stone. I'd have made a decent landing."

For the first time the policeman laughed. "That's a fair enough answer. So that's how you cracked your head?"

Mrs. Rich was about to say something, then she looked across at Ross. He felt bad about his mother. She would have been decent and there need never have been all this explaining. He hated having to explain.

As if reading his thoughts the policeman said, "You'd have saved the police a lot of trouble, and your parents here, if you'd come out with the truth earlier on, my lad. Now it seems we have another of the family in it and neither of you of much help. Did you notice anything on the building site, any-thing unusual?"

"No, I was a bit stunned, and I wanted to get to school. There's a loose board in the back fence. It was nearest so I got through there."

"And Peter here heard nothing of that sound, in fact only walked all round the building site, or probably ran. Very well." At last they knew he was going. Mr. Rich escorted him to the door, and they listened to the goodnights and the closing of the front door. Mr. Rich came back into the dining-room.

"Of all the stupid things, Ross. How can you expect them to believe anything that either you or Peter has to say now?"

"Sorry, Dad." He wanted to be alone, away from their accusations. "And you were late home today; very late. What were you up to?"

Mr. Rich worked at the Town Hall and had arrived home just before Ross. Ross's heart sank. He thought of Mr. Wilson, the warmth of the conservatory; it was his secret—his and Jeff's. Then he recalled Mr. Wilson's words, "God knows you fell to the ground, too", the foreign accent, the something interesting about him.

"I'm waiting." And indeed they were all waiting and watching. Reluctantly Ross took the blue paper from his blazer pocket and handed it to his father; the room was very quiet now.

"You went here, to this place?" Mr. Rich tapped the paper with his left hand.

"Yes."

"Well, I think that's pretty good—what I call initiative. I gather this is what you told Mum about last week. You must tell me more about it some time, Ross."

Ross stared at his father, then held out his hand for the precious paper.

"What's the lark now?" asked Peter, trying not to show too much interest.

"A scientific project of some importance." Mr. Rich handed the paper to Peter, while Ross waited jealously.

Carol bent over Peter's shoulder, frowning at the paper. "Wow, you're a sly one, Ross." She grinned at him. He leant across the table and grabbed the paper, then made for the door.

CHAPTER TEN

TEA IN THE ATTIC

The next day, Ross and Jeff sat either end of the table in the attic room. Outside, the rain fell relentlessly and it was on account of this that they were unable to have their usual excursion to Simms Wood. Brooding over the mysterious affair at the building site, they cupped their chins in their hands, resting their elbows on the table, their feet hooked round the legs of the old wooden chairs. Jeff liked it in this room, tucked away from the rest of the house. Sometimes on a Saturday Mrs. Rich would bring them glasses of orange squash and cakes she had just baked; and they would sit lazily sucking the cool drink through transparent straws. Like Ross, Jeff wished to arrange his own life, to have time, loads of time to do just as he pleased.

The door opened, and they both turned. Mrs. Rich saw their heads outlined against the attic window. "Jeff," she said, "would you like me to phone your mother and ask if you could stay to tea? It's raining so hard, you'll get soaked again. You really ought to have gone straight home instead of coming down here in this rain."

Jeff's face lit up. "Yes, please, Mrs. Rich."

"And you could have tea up here for a bit of fun, eh?"

Ross didn't look up, but Jeff pushed back his chair cheerfully. "What we having?"

Mrs. Rich laughed. "Well, if you put the light on you might be able to see." But even in the half light she could make out Ross's downcast expression. "I'll go and phone, and then in about ten minutes you can both come down and fetch the trays."

"Thanks, Mrs. Rich," said Jeff.

Ross knew his mother was making it easy for him; breakfast had been an awkward meal, and he had not been looking forward to another session with Peter facing him across the table.

"Ask my mum how long I can stay," pleaded Jeff.

"I'll do that." She was gone.

"You reckon the ten minutes, Ross." Always at Sampson's things went by the clock—time for the shop to open, time for the second batch of bread, time to sweep the shop, time to get up. Jeff sat down again, leaning across the table, so that he could keep an eye on Ross's wrist watch. His life was divided in two parts—the part that belonged to the bakery, where they needed him, and where he would not willingly do anything to make things difficult; and the part that he and Ross shared, when they schemed or idled, when they planned the most impossible things freely, because there was no one to criticise or comment if their plans came to nothing.

Ross switched on the light. The thought of a meal on their own helped him to banish Peter from his thoughts.

"Hope I can stay," said Jeff, remembering that sometimes at the shop he was needed to do odd jobs. "Ross, I thought about something."

"What?"

"Well, you know you said that policeman had things down in his notebook, and he said it was the little things that fitted in and gave him a clue. Why don't you and me put everything down? Guess we could work something out." It was another of their plans which would probably lead to nothing, but which would be exciting while it lasted.

"Bet we could," agreed Ross.

"Is it ten minutes yet?" enquired Jeff.

"No."

"But we can go down and fetch the things now, and then do the list afterwards." They made for the door, and a little later returned slowly in a procession, Jeff with the tray of food, halting every now and again to inspect its contents, Ross with the crockery, and Mrs. Rich with the tea and milk.

The room looked twice as cheerful after they had laid the tea.

"You going to play *Scrabble* or *Monopoly* afterwards?" questioned Mrs. Rich.

"We're not playing games," replied Jeff; "we've got something special to do."

"Sounds serious," she laughed.

Ross straightened the plates, still avoiding his mother's glance.

"What time've I got to go?" asked Jeff.

"Mr. Rich will run you home at half past seven; he's got a meeting at eight o'clock, so that will fit in quite well."

"Aw, thanks." Jeff relaxed, with a sense of freedom. Hours—well, nearly three—in which he and Ross could do as they liked.

The rain beat against the window that looked out onto the building site, as the two shared the last piece of cake. Ross pushed the empty tea-things to one side, then fetched a biro and exercise book from his cupboard.

"Don't forget it's the little things," grinned Jeff.

Ross opened the book at the middle; this way the double pages provided ample room for all the information they could collect, with the advantage that it could be viewed together.

"I'll put that down at the top." Ross recalled that evening vividly, when the policeman had slowly pronounced his opinion about the value of the little things. He wrote in large letters across the top of the two pages, 'It's the little things'.

"Now, we're only putting down things we're dead certain about."

"What you going to put first?"

Ross grinned, then began writing slowly. 'Ross Rich seen entering building site, Tuesday morning between 8.30 and 8.45 a.m.' He read the entry out to Jeff.

"What you put that first for?"

"Dunno; just thought I would." Once more he began to write. 'Sound of smashing heard just before 11.45 on Monday evening, coming from direction of building site.' And again, 'Peter came home very late, quarter to twelve. He came by the back path. He didn't come through the garden gate because, he said, it was locked. But it wasn't locked, so he was lying.'

"That's three things," encouraged Jeff; but suddenly there seemed so little information available. "Did he say what was stolen?"

"Some valuable tools; and there was something else the matter, but he sort of shut up then." Ross pondered the matter. Downstairs they were probably discussing him, how he'd been found out, while up here he and Jeff were trying to probe the whole mystery. He re-read his last entry. "Guess the owl would have heard Pete; guess he never went down that path at all."

Ross frowned. He closed his mind to his own lies of the past. The thing was, you could never tell with Peter. Sometimes he just put on airs and pretended to make you think he was important or knew about special things. Peter's sort were like that, just to make sure you didn't think they were kids any more.

"Someone coming," whispered Jeff.

"S'pect it's Mum for the washing up."

CHAPTER ELEVEN

THE SECRET IS OUT

But it was not Mrs. Rich, but Peter who held the door ajar while Carol pushed past into the room.

"Hi, Jeff," she greeted, sauntering across to the fire. She crouched by its small warmth, spreading her hands in front of its red glow, while her emerald green jersey made a splash of colour in the room. And all the time Peter watched Ross, Ross who looked so guilty.

"You can knock when you come in," snapped Ross.

"Oh, come off it," laughed Carol.

Peter closed the door, and came across to sit on the edge of the bed. "I've been thinking." He pushed back his fair hair, then sat staring down at the floor for a while. "It's like this." Now he eyed the two at the table. "There's things we each know. What about we get together?"

Ross waited. If Peter meant, you tell me what you know, and then I'll decide afterwards whether I tell you anything, then he wasn't interested.

"You see, if we could, well, trace who the culprit is, without my having to get my friend involved——"

"It would be marvellous if we could prove Pete and his friend had nothing to do with the robbery," said Carol.

Ross felt a surge of excitement at the prospect of engaging in detective work with Peter and Carol; with them it could be the real thing.

"What were you doing?" Carol came across to the table. "Let's have a look."

For a moment Ross hesitated. Why had Peter decided to ask for help? Peter seemed to fill the room, his feet splayed out on the square of blue carpet, his bulky black jersey, his large hands. "It's O.K. by me and Jeff," Ross said at last. "Anyway, we were making a list ourselves.

Peter stretched himself on the bed, his hands on his head. "What've you got on your list?"

Jeff and Ross glanced at each other. Should they read them out to him? He would certainly get a nasty surprise at one of them.

"I went across the road before tea," said Carol, "to find out if anyone could have seen you on the fence. Well, no one could have seen you from the road, so it was either Mrs. Hammond next door——"

"No it wasn't."

"Why not?"

"Because she'd have had to see me through a tree trunk," retorted Ross.

"Sharp, aren't you?" laughed Peter.

"Then it must have been Mrs. Wright, opposite; she could have seen you from the upstairs window. It looks right along our fence. Funny she didn't seem to think you fell off the fence."

Ross realised Carol was hinting that he had intended going on the building site, and he was angry. "Well, that's too bad. Anyway, Pete never tried to get in through the garden gate."

"Who says?" Peter sat up and stared at Ross.

"I do. The gate wasn't locked or bolted."

"Don't play around; of course it was bolted."

Ross explained how he knew Peter was deceiving them.

"Whew, you kids! O.K., you win," he admitted.

"Why didn't you try the gate? Weren't you down there?" enquired Jeff. Peter changed the subject. "Did you see anything when you did a crash landing over the fence?"

Ross remembered the words, 'It's the small things.' Suppose, in those few moments on the building site, there was one thing he had seen which would fit into the puzzle and solve the mystery! He tried to recapture the scene.

"Well, at first, when I was still standing on the fence, there was a pile of broken tiles and bricks."

"You already told our copper about that. Anything else?" Peter tried not to show too much concern.

"Well, after I'd fallen over, when I opened my eyes I was facing the other way, and I could see the backs of the boards they've put to make the front fence. One had that advertisement for Wonderloaf, only it was upside down."

"That's not much help."

"And the barrier was open, and——"

Peter sat up sharply. "The barrier was open?"

"Yes, and a lorry was backed into the entrance."

"Look, I don't want a lot of fairy tales you've cooked up."

"It's not me that's lying. I saw the lorry backed in; it was—well, I'm pretty certain it was a double wheel base truck, and it had brown paint. But when the man came round the side, I got scared and ducked down behind a bush."

"That's all impossible," insisted Peter.

"Course it's not," argued Jeff; "they open at eight, same as we do."

"But, my dear children, there was a strike, a one-day token strike. Didn't you notice there was no one around on Tuesday, or did the blow on your head deprive you of your senses?"

"The gate was open, and I saw a truck, and a man," insisted Ross.

"You're absolutely dead certain?" Peter was now taking him seriously. "What was the man like?"

"I—I'm not sure, except that he had a whitish peaked cap."

"You know, you might have hit on something." Peter began to pace the floor. Ross and Jeff exchanged excited glances.

"How d'you know there was a strike?" queried Ross.

"What's that matter?"

"The policeman didn't say anything about it." Ross hated being fobbed off with excuses.

"There's a lot of things he didn't mention," observed Peter. "Say, Carol, I wonder if Mrs. Wright saw anything of this lorry?"

"If she saw Ross go over the fence, you bet she tried to see what he was up to, anyway."

"Then she'd have seen him lying there all knocked out," said Jeff.

Carol laughed. "She'd have come dashing over to Mum, and Ross would have been for it. No, I don't reckon she could see a thing, and the gate's too far round the corner up the road for her to see."

"Then the chances are the policeman doesn't know anything about it—yet. So that means——" Peter stopped abruptly, clasped his hands and blew through his fingers. "But if that lorry bit is correct——"

"Of course it is," declared Jeff loyally.

"I must work this out. At least we know someone else besides us two was on the site between——"

"So you were there that night." Sharp as a knife Ross was on to his brother.

Peter rounded on him. "Can't you mind your own business!"

"What was the strike about?" Carol tried to smooth things over, to stop the quarrel.

"You wouldn't understand," he replied scornfully.

"What were you there for?" pursued Ross, now suspicious of Peter's motives.

"Look, I'm not saying anything." Peter plunged his hands in his pockets, then made for the door.

Carol shrugged her shoulders.

"What's Peter been up to?" asked Ross.

"I don't know." She looked put out, and Ross wondered what had happened between them, that now Peter wanted to leave her out.

E

CHAPTER TWELVE

SOMETHING HIDDEN

The record-player was pulsing out the rhythm, but against the background of beat music Peter was restless. The way Ross had caught him out yesterday, the way he had betrayed himself, had unnerved him. He turned off the music and crossed to the window which looked out onto the front garden, then began drumming with his fingers on the window-sill. Pursued by his fears, he could settle to nothing. He heard the whining sound that the rusty iron gate made on its hinges, and to his dismay saw Ross entering—not Ross on his own as he usually was on his belated return from school, but Ross accompanied by the policeman. Peter drew back against the curtains, terrified of what was going to happen next. But the two strange companions did not proceed up to the front door, nor by the path that led to the back door to the kitchen. Instead Ross was leading the way along the front hedge followed by the policeman.

He stopped, peering into the laurel bushes. The next moment the burly policeman also bent over to investigate. There was Ross, with his skinny form and untidy raincoat, his lank fair hair surmounted by the school cap which, owing to many soakings, had shrunk too much to fit his head. And there beside him was the expansive policeman, navy uniform and smart helmet. Something hidden by the dusty laurel leaves fascinated them both, and Peter watching anxiously was irritated by their attitude. What had the policeman come for? What was he really looking for? Not a bird's nest, but something else, and Ross, the little idiot, was probably feeling cocky because he had got the chance of showing off one of his finds. Hadn't he got the sense to know that not everyone was interested in birds' nests, and owls and grass snakes? Didn't it occur to him that the policeman was looking for bigger stakes than a sparrow's nest? He watched them straighten up, Ross looking mightily pleased with himself; then to his surprise the policeman went out of the front gate, leaving Ross in the garden. Peter set the record-player going again, then crept downstairs. He could hear the chink of china in the kitchen, then his mother asking Ross something.

"I just showed him that nest in the hedge," answered Ross.

"Showed who?" That was Carol.

"The policeman, silly; you should listen. He was patrolling past the building site when I came home, so he walked down with me and he asked me if I'd found many birds' nests in the garden."

"So you couldn't miss that chance," laughed Carol. "As if he was interested!"

"Of course he was. Anyway, he knows quite a lot about them."

"Did he say anything else?" asked Mrs. Rich.

"Well, I told him about me—you know, about my drawings; and he said he'd like to see them sometime."

"So you invited him to come and see you."
Carol's voice was a bit sharp.

"What's wrong with that? Guess what he asked
about you?"

Peter heard Carol laugh again.

"He wanted to know if you and Pete were any
good at drawing, and I said you couldn't draw for
nuts."

"Well, of all the cheek!"

"And what did you say about Peter?" asked
Mrs. Rich.

"I said he was jolly good, and he was going to be
an architect. Then he said he'd got to be going, so
I came in."

On the stairs, Peter turned and went back to his
room. He heard Ross go past whistling cheerfully.
Why couldn't he keep his mouth shut! Why must
he always get himself mixed up in what was nothing
to do with him! Had Ross said more than that to
the policeman? He heard Carol shouting that tea
was ready, but he stayed in his room, while the
music went on and on.

CHAPTER THIRTEEN

THE LITTLE THINGS

After school on Friday, Ross strolled home with Jeff. It was the one day that Jeff was supposed to be home on time, since Friday evening was occupied with the many odd jobs and preparations that would save precious time on Saturday. When they reached the High Street, they pushed their way through the crowds, discussing their plans, then turned into the passage that led to the back of Sampson's shop, for the last moments together.

"Two o'clock at my place," said Ross once more.

"O.K." Jeff released his satchel from his back, anticipating the freedom of their expedition to the Old Barn.

"Jeff, your mum wants you." It was Miss Rogers who helped in the shop on Fridays and Saturdays, calling from the back door.

"Coming," answered Jeff. "See you tomorrow, Ross."

Ross waited till he had gone indoors. As he was about to make his way back into the High Street, the Sampson's delivery van turned into the passage, blocking the exit. Ross stood to one side of the yard, watching its slow approach, its lurching movement over the bumpy ground. It was a cream thirty-hundred-weight van with blue lettering on the sides, and was fitted inside with shelves and trays for bread and pastries.

"Hullo, kid," hailed the driver, getting down from the cab. Leaving the engine running, he went across to open the garage door. There were three garages at the side of the yard, which at one time had been stables for the horses that were used then.

Ross regarded the dusty lettering on the van— Wm. Sampson, Baker and pastry cook, High Street, Hamstorth, and Market Lane, Weststorth.

The driver whistled as he tugged at the ill-fitting door, then once more got into the van and began straightening up in order to back into the garage. First he drove into the far corner by the bake-house, then leant out of the window as he backed slowly towards the waiting garage, aware of Ross's critical gaze. Ross reckoned he wouldn't make it that time. He looked from the garage to the van, calculating the angle; and sure enough the driver went forward once more for a second attempt. Ross leant against the wall, facing the open garage, and it was in that moment that he caught sight of something that made him start. Now he no longer noticed the throbbing engine, the confident whistling of the driver, nor the clatter from the bake-house at the end of the yard. Everything seemed far away; only the thing there loomed large and frightening. Meanwhile the van backed slowly, finally blotting it out, but nothing could erase it from Ross's mind. He went on staring. The driver slammed the cab door, emerged from the darkness of the garage and prepared to close the wooden doors. With a kick of his foot he thrust the thing further inside, then padlocked the doors.

Ross ran out of the yard, trying to escape from the thing he had seen. In that one moment everything had changed. If only it had been somewhere else, anywhere but Jeff's. Now things could never be the same with him and Jeff; nothing would ever be the same, because he couldn't possibly talk about it with Jeff. The headline of their page of clues had been the policeman's 'It's the little things', and now perhaps it was coming true, but not in the way he and Jeff had expected. Well, he wouldn't tell, not anyone; if Peter wouldn't tell what he knew, then neither would he.

All during tea, he avoided Peter's enquiring glance. Yesterday Peter had been avoiding Ross's cheeky look, but now it was Ross who was uncomfortable. Eventually he escaped with the excuse that he wanted to do some drawing.

For a long time he gazed out of the window to the distant trees of Simms Wood, the place of secrets, but the sight of the dark barrier on the horizon did not excite him. Tomorrow was to have been one of their 'special' days; now it offered no fun. But it wasn't only the sense of disappointment regarding the outing; it was the ugly fear that tormented him, the fear that things would never be the same again. It was no good pretending it didn't matter, or that he had never seen that evidence.

Dejected, he sat down at the table with the exercise book spread out in front of him. He wanted to pull the offending pages out and tear them up. Instead, he toyed with his biro, then on the empty right-hand page began sketching a flag, first an oblong then the stars, small five-pointed shapes, then stripes. He remembered it all so vividly. It was almost the first thing he saw when he opened his eyes that morning—a ragged American flag tied to the load that was protruding from the back of the lorry—yet until he had been confronted with the same emblem in the garage, it had remained at the back of his mind, something of no great importance. Even if he wanted to tell anyone about it, they probably wouldn't believe him; they'd say he was imagining things. But he knew, he knew the moment he saw the crumpled flag in Sampson's, that it was the same one, and try as he would to shut the picture out of his mind, he could not. He saw it now, lying at the side of the garage, as though discarded after some trip, one corner narrowed, the corner that must have been drawn together to tie on that load.

The thing was, what should he do? If he asked Jeff about it, Jeff would think he was trying to accuse his father, especially as in the first place he had not mentioned that the piece of material tied on the load was an American flag. And Jeff hated rows and arguments. Then he remembered what Mr. Wilson had said about knowing he fell off the fence. If God knew about that, and minded, then He must know about this afternoon, because what happened this afternoon was a lot worse than slipping on that loose board last week. Ross kept quite still, gazing at the drawing with its stars and stripes. He wasn't very sure how to ask God about anything, even though he'd been going to Junior Church with Jeff for a long time. It was because of Jeff he went in the first place, but mostly he didn't take a lot of notice, his mind full of their next exploit. He closed his eyes; it seemed the right thing to do if he was going to pray. "Please God, will you do something about Jeff and me. Don't let anything happen so as me and Jeff won't be friends any more. Amen."

The room was getting darker; there was not even the glow from the electric fire, for in his musing Ross had forgotten to switch it on. He got onto his bed and kneeled up at the window, looking out at the lime tree and the building site beyond. He could hear Peter's record-player—the same records night after night. Why should he tell Peter what he had seen? If anyone found out that Peter had been snooping round on the building site, then Pete would have to fend for himself. He couldn't tell on Jeff; he *couldn't*.

And then he knew the right thing to do. Tomorrow morning he would go and see Mr. Wilson; it wouldn't make any difference to the afternoon outing. Mr. Wilson would know the best thing to do about Jeff.

He ran downstairs, suddenly light-hearted, colliding with Carol.

"Tell old Pete to turn it off," he shouted, then disappeared down the second flight of stairs.

CHAPTER FOURTEEN

IN NEED OF HELP

"Can I go to Jeff's?" Ross tried to make his voice sound casual. Peter eyed his brother across the breakfast table. He, too, was afraid—afraid lest Ross was up to something.

"But I thought it was this afternoon you were going out with him," objected Mrs. Rich.

"Yes, I know, Mum; but we just want to——" Ross hesitated. He was lying. He'd asked God to help, and it didn't seem right to begin by deceiving his mother.

"You mean you just can't stay away from one another for five minutes." Mr. Rich was hidden behind the newspaper.

"Can't see what you see in each other," added Peter, turning his knife over and over, impatient for the moment when his father would have finished with the paper.

"Well, I can't see what you see in——"

Peter looked up, fear tormenting him again.

"Ross!" reproved Mrs. Rich. "You can go when you've helped clear the table, but don't make a nuisance of yourselves at the bakery. Jeff's mum and dad have a lot to do on Saturday."

"We won't," assured Ross cheerfully, collecting the plates with a great clatter.

"So long, Mum." Ross ran out into Lewis Road. Almost opposite was Mrs. Wright's house, an unwelcome reminder that all his doings were not so secret as he imagined. He had come this way instead of through the road at the rear of the houses, so as to make it appear that he really was going to see Jeff. Once at the end of Lewis Road, he got onto the back road, then made his way through the little park to Simms Wood and onto Wicket Lane. He began to run, the April air fresh through his hair; not even Simms Wood had been able to entice him, so anxious was he to listen to Mr. Wilson's solution of his difficulty. Outside the Old Barn he stopped, breathless. It was not so easy on his own, without Jeff to egg him on. Even though there was little sunlight, the stretch of ground ahead seemed to catch all the light and warmth of the spring morning.

Ross went in slowly, but this time the conservatory was empty. There was no sign of Mr. Wilson. Somehow Ross had banked on his being around. The back door to the house was ajar. Ross approached it cautiously, and knocked. Peering into the old-fashioned kitchen, with its great dresser stacked with blue crockery, he saw Mr. Wilson sitting at the table and watching him over his spectacles.

"Hullo, Mr. Wilson."

"You are very early." Mr. Wilson got up slowly and came across to the door. "You and Jeff have come this morning instead of this afternoon. Yes?" Again the foreign accent intrigued Ross.

"Oh no, it's not that, Mr. Wilson; you see—we

are still coming this afternoon. Jeff isn't with me now."

"So you have come this morning also." Mr. Wilson was standing beside Ross. "You are in trouble. We'll go to my office; that is always a very good place for sorting out problems. Some places are, you know."

Ross followed him to the outhouse. There was the bench just as he remembered it, the filing cabinet, the exciting array of nets and charts. Mr. Wilson lowered himself into the wooden chair, so that he was facing Ross, and just where the sun, streaming in through the window, warmed the two of them.

"You sit on the bench, Ross." Mr. Wilson shifted some of the papers to one side. He picked up some unravelled rope. "I use this to trap them sometimes. They are looking for pieces to make their nests. Now what were you going to tell me?"

Ross hesitated. It was going to be so easy, but now he realised it was impossible to relate the one incident—it wouldn't make sense.

"It is a long story." Mr. Wilson spread his hands expressively. "Most troubles are long stories, Ross, so it is best to begin at the beginning, the very beginning. You think that is a good idea?"

Ross, sitting on the bench, swung his legs to and fro. He saw no other way out of it. So, beginning with the owl at night and the sound of Peter's homecoming, he retailed each detail, and all the time Mr. Wilson listened intently, at times cocking his head to one side as though to consider some knotty problems. For a few moments after Ross had concluded his story, Mr. Wilson was silent.

Then, looking directly at Ross, he said, "And you are certain it is the same flag? Yes, I see you are quite, quite certain."

"Yes."

"And you don't know what to do about it?"

"No."

"And you have not told anyone at all except me?"

"No."

"Now, I do not know what is the right thing to do about it, either—not yet—because of Jeff. He is your friend, and he is my friend, and we would not want to harm him. So as we do not know what to do, we could pretend it did not happen. But then you and Jeff would never be real friends any more —you know that?"

"But I wouldn't ever stop being friends with Jeff," declared Ross.

"All the same it would not be quite the same, because you would be hiding something. Jeff would suggest you thought of some more clues, and you would say, No. And he would say, Why not? And you would argue, give some excuse, and all the time it would be because of that flag you saw at the bakery."

"I see," said Ross dejectedly.

"And you do not want to tell Jeff what you saw."

"Oh no." Ross was very definite about that.

"Then I will tell you what I will do. I am going to ask God, our heavenly Father, to help us, to show us what to do, and I am sure by the time you and Jeff get here this afternoon He will have shown us the right thing to do. Now, I want you to cheer up. Why, if you hadn't found that blackbird the other morning, I shouldn't have known you and Jeff, and I shouldn't have been able to help."

"How do you know God will tell us what to do?"

"Because He's been telling me for a very long time. When I wasn't much older than you, that was when I was Alexander Wilenski—you see, I have a new, British name now—we had to leave our country. My brother Joseph, he was younger and he did not mind, but I was very frightened and very angry because we were refugees. And I told Him about being afraid and angry, and, well, I had my answer. And there are the fine things in England, and we are not afraid any more; and I am not angry any more."

"I didn't tell Mum I was coming here," said Ross sudenly.

"No, you said to her, 'I am going to see Jeff.' So when you go home, you will pretend you have been with Jeff, and you will say, 'Oh yes, we had a good time; we went to Simms Wood', and all the time you have not been with Jeff."

Ross felt the colour rising to his cheeks. It was all so true.

"And all the time your mother will know you have not been with Jeff."

"How?"

"She will know you are not honest with her. She will know you are pretending. Everyone likes their secrets, but that does not mean lying. But about the flag, I am sure God understands you cannot tell; you are not sure what to do. So wait till this afternoon."

Ross slid down from the bench.

"Pretending is lying," went on Mr. Wilson. "It is what we try to do with God. He says we are sinners; and we say, no we are quite all right, and we build up a wall between us and Him, and we cannot break it down. That is why the Lord Jesus gave His life on the cross—to break down that wall of sin and pretence. I think you could ask Him to forgive you and trust Him to do that. And then, well, you ask Him about the pretending at home. I will see you and Jeff this afternoon, eh?"

CHAPTER FIFTEEN

THE ANSWER

Ross walked home very slowly, lingering in Simms Wood in order to put off the time of his return. Here was the haunt of the owl who by its call on that particular night had started this whole train of events. And yet he had never seen the owl here; perhaps he and Jeff could stay here till dusk one day and watch for the owl. Then the joyous thought of an evening expedition with Jeff was dimmed by the shadow of recent events. Alone, he began to pray, "Please God will you make it all right for me and Jeff. I won't pretend and tell lies any more, if only you'll let it still be the same between us." Then he remembered what Mr. Wilson had said. "And please will you make it all right between You and me and forgive me because of Jesus." It didn't sound quite like a prayer, but it was what he wanted to ask.

He entered by the back gate, stayed for a few moments in the shed, then went indoors. In the kitchen his mother was cutting rounds of pastry, and all Ross's brave intentions dwindled, there was so much explaining to do.

"Ross." It was the tone of her voice that warned him his mother was upset and a bit angry.

"Yes." Fingering the crinkled edges of the pastry

he waited.

"Mrs. Sampson just rang up."

Ross started. "I—I didn't go round to Jeff's."

"I know you didn't." Mrs. Rich looked straight at Ross. "It isn't that I mind your not going there, but you never meant to go there, did you?"

"Not really; no, I didn't."

"Then why did you have to say that was where you were going, just because you thought no one would ask any questions?"

"I wanted to go and see Mr. Wilson about something, before I went with Jeff."

"Well, Jeff won't be going with you at all."

"Oh Mum, why not?" He was alarmed. It was a cruel punishment. But his mother laughed. "He's got German measles."

Ross stared at her. "But we were going specially——"

"Not Jeff, not for a few days."

Ross frowned. That was a funny way for God to answer Mr. Wilson's prayer. The odd thing was that Mr. Wilson didn't know about it yet, and he did, and it was Mr. Wilson's prayer.

"Mum, I can go this afternoon, can't I?"

"You don't deserve to."

"No. I suppose I don't."

"But you can go; only, Ross, no more lies; you don't expect me to treat you that way."

"Oh no. Anyway, I wasn't going to any more. Mr. Wilson said something about—you know——"

"What did he say?"

Ross smoothed the flour on the pastry board. "He

F

said telling lies was like building a wall between yourself and the other person, the same as—Mum, how long will Jeff be away?"

"Bit more than a week, I expect."

"What's for dinner?"

"Roast lamb and mince pie."

He went out into the hall. Peter was leaning against the wall, his hands in his pockets, and Ross was suddenly angry that his brother had overheard the conversation in the kitchen.

"What d'you want?"

"Nothing particular; just wondering if you'd made any more breath-taking discoveries," answered Peter lazily.

"You were listening; you're a rotten spy. I wouldn't tell you, anyway." He said the words without thinking of what he had seen the previous evening.

"Oh, so you have unearthed something?"

Then Ross remembered. But it wouldn't be that sort of thing Peter meant. Peter was afraid of something concerning himself. Ross made for the stairs.

"Oh, come off it, Rossy; don't be so dumb," coaxed Peter, but Ross was offended. Alone in his room, he spread the exercise book on the table, and scanned the few entries. Should he add the evidence seen in the garage at the bakery? He began to consider Mr. Wilson's words about God answering prayer. God had helped him to be honest with his mother, when he was thinking it was too difficult; so, in a way, the telephone call had answered two prayers. He tore a sheet from the back of the exercise book and began writing to Jeff.

"Dear Jeff,

"Going to the O.B. this afternoon. I will tell
Mr. Wilson about the German measles. I will
write to you again and tell you about the O.B.
School will be rotten on Monday. I will tell Mr.
Forbes about you. Hurry up and come back.
Mum says I have had G.M. so that is O.K. I hope.
                    "Signed R.R.
"P.S. what about 31265R for our code number?"

CHAPTER SIXTEEN

WAITING

Ross pocketed his letter, and made his way to the High Street. Outside Sampson's bakery he hesitated, not knowing whether to leave the letter with Mrs. Sampson or whether to go round to the back door. Seeing Mrs. Sampson was busy, he went down the side of the shop to the yard. It was un-usually quiet, and two of the three garages were open, but the third which had revealed the startling clue was closed. Now Ross observed that, although there were three doors, the interior was one large garage, so that if he were to go across and peer in he might even see that tattered flag once more. But the sense that this was Jeff's home deterred him, together with the knowledge that if anyone asked him what he was looking for he would have to tell the truth, and not another lie.

Jeff's room was just above the back door and next to it with corner windows was the Sampsons' sitting-room. Ross had only been in it once, but it was strangely exciting having a sitting-room that looked down onto a yard, that kept watch on all that was going on. He gave a shrill whistle, then, on receiving no reply, picked up a small pebble and threw it at Jeff's window. Still there was no response, so he aimed another stone at the sitting-room window. Jeff's face appeared above the sill. When he saw Ross he pushed at the ill-fitting sash. Ross exhibited the letter, and just then Mr. Sampson came from the bakehouse. Taking the letter from Ross, he screwed it into a ball and aimed it at the open window.

"Thanks, Dad," said Jeff.

"Now you get along, son," Mr. Sampson was half-ordering Ross.

"O.K., Mr. Sampson. See you, Jeff."

It was nearly three o'clock when once more he entered the Old Barn, and this time Mr. Wilson was standing waiting by the outhouse that he called his office and ringing station.

"Jeff is not with you?" he looked surprised.

"Guess what? He's got German measles."

A slow smile spread over Mr. Wilson's face. "He has the German measles. So he has the German measles." He nodded his head thoughtfully, and Ross couldn't help laughing that he found the whole business of Jeff's misfortune so amusing.

"You see, I was sure God would have an answer for us, and it is the German measles. Mind you, He only tells you a bit at a time, and this is enough to be going on with."

"You mean you didn't know what to do about Jeff until——"

"No, but it was in good time, the answer. Now I think perhaps I should keep the things I was going to show you until Jeff is with us again. You wouldn't be very pleased if it was you had the German measles and I showed Jeff the things."

"No, not really." Still, Ross was disappointed at

the delay.

Ross had almost forgotten to relate how he had learned of Jeff's illness. "Jeff's mum phoned up while I was with you this morning."

"And your mother was not at all pleased that you had not told her the truth."

"No."

"But you have made a fresh start; you have owned up."

"Mr. Wilson, how do people know when something's not the right thing to do?"

"Now you are talking about Ross Rich. I think God has always let you know in good time when something is wrong, in plenty of time for you to ask Him to help you if you are finding it difficult."

Ross grinned. "Guess so."

"Now you have to be quite honest with Peter, too, and he has to be honest with you. But, like you, he has got himself into a bit of trouble by telling untruths. And the policeman will not be very pleased about that."

"What are we going to do, Mr. Wilson?"

"Ross, I am not very sure. You have a big problem. If you tell of what you saw at the bakery, you might help your brother, but you would feel bad about Jeff."

"You mean if I tell Pete."

"Yes, or your parents."

"But then I'd have to tell on Pete if I told Mum and Dad anything and he'd be mad at me. I don't want to tell on Pete."

"Nor on Jeff."

"No."

"So," Mr. Wilson spread his hands out and shrugged his shoulders, "we ask the right things to do, and how to do it."

"You mean God can really answer things like that?"

"Certainly, and we must not hide the truth."

"But I don't want to tell on anyone."

"No, perhaps not; so we wait for God to make the next move; we wait for things to show us the way. Now you go home, and tomorrow I shall look for you in church, and we will remember about asking for directions, eh?"

"O.K. So long, Mr. Wilson. I'll be at church."

CHAPTER SEVENTEEN

BRAZILIAN OR BRITISH

"Mum——" Ross hesitated a moment, wondering what his parents would think of his request. "Mum, can I borrow a Bible this morning?"

Mr. Rich, who was cleaning the shoes by the kitchen door which opened onto the garden, turned to look at Ross. "There's the copy of the New English Bible that I got for Carol for school. It's still on the bottom shelf of the bookcase."

"Will she be mad if I take it?"

"Since it's been lying there for the last few weeks, I should think it would be a good idea if someone used it."

"O.K., Dad. Ross went into the front room to inspect the bookcase, and there, sure enough, was the brand new copy of the Bible in its orange dust-jacket. Back in the hall he struggled into his rain-coat, tucked the Bible under his arm, and ran out into Lewis Road. Despite his hurry, the service had already begun by the time he reached the church in the High Street. He made his way up the aisle to where some of the boys sat on the right-hand side, then he looked round to see if he could locate Mr. Wilson.

"No Jeff?" questioned the leader in a whisper.

"He's got German measles," answered Ross, trying to balance the Bible on the narrow book ledge.

During the prayer he bowed his head, out of habit, but did not close his eyes. Instead, he inspected the younger boys in the row in front, till once more the thought came to him about pretending. He closed his eyes and tried to take notice of the prayer, but the collar of his raincoat was irritating his neck, and his mind wandered. When they filed into the classroom at the rear of the church, he was still thinking how difficult it was not to pretend about things. In the room there was the usual commotion, the clattering of chairs, the jostling of each other, making out that this was all very necessary before settling down, and Ross enjoyed every bit of it, calculating how long one could go on.

Instead of their normal lesson time, the leader introduced a visitor, a bronzed young man who recounted the new and exciting things taking place in Brazil. Yet, even though Ross was intrigued by all that he said, by the man himself, his thoughts escaped to Simms Wood and Jeff, to the Old Barn and Mr. Wilson.

"Now what about you telling me something," the man demanded suddenly. Ross made an effort to come back from his thoughts, from the things which were so pleasant because they made no demands on him, because they always went along with his own inclinations.

"Tell me this. Would you take me for a Brazilian?"

"They don't dress like that," said the boy next to Ross.

"Oh yes, quite a lot of them do. All the same, we could do something about that." He produced a gay sombrero, and they laughed as he placed it carefully on his head. "That better? Am I a Brazilian now?"

"Your name's only Williams, so you couldn't be a Brazilian—not with that name." Ross couldn't see who was speaking.

"Well, that's easy enough. People can change their names, you know. Suppose I choose something like Don Mario——"

"But you aren't one, are you, sir?" interrupted Ross.

"No, I'm not, am I," Mr. Williams admitted quietly; "I'm trying to make you think I am, because I know a bit about Brazil, and because I'm dark-skinned and dark-haired. Is there any way I can really be a Brazilian? Isn't there anything I can do?" Now he was looking straight at Ross.

Ross was thinking hard. "You weren't born one, were you, sir?"

"No, that's the trouble; I wasn't born a Brazilian. I wasn't born in Brazil. Now suppose you find something for me in that new Bible I see you've got with you. Gospel of John——" Ross began to thumb the pages feverishly, while several others declared they had already found the place.

"Chapter one and verse twelve," encouraged the speaker.

At length Ross had it.

"Read it out."

With his finger following the print, Ross read the words slowly. "But to all who did receive him, to those who have yielded him their allegiance, he gave the right to become children of God."

"That's it. Now, it so happens, I can be made a Brazilian, though I'm not born one. Under certain conditions the government of Brazil is willing to receive me as one of her citizens. But here's the difficulty: I have to give up being British; I can't possibly be both—it has to be one or the other. Now God promises that if we receive Jesus, His Son, in our hearts, if we give Him our allegiance and trust the Lord Jesus to forgive our sin—you know He died on the cross for that—then He will make us citizens of heaven, members of His family. But we have to leave off the old connections; we can't belong to the Lord Jesus and to the devil. Now, Brazil might not fancy having me as one of their nation; but God says anyone may come to Him, boys and girls as well; everyone who believes what He has promised, and accepts it, may belong to His family. Some people pretend they belong— when I'm in Brazil I like them to think I'm a Brazilian—but these people have never asked to be taken into God's family; they still belong to the old master. They're a bit like me: I would like to be Brazilian, if I could still be British, but I have to choose which one I want. God says it's the same for us; we have to choose."

From the church came the sound of the closing hymn. Ross's finger was still on the words in the Gospel of John. He thought of Mr. Wilson, who had changed his nationality, changed his land, changed his name from Alexander Wilenski to Alexander Wilson; Mr. Wilson, who had done just what this sentence in the New Testament said —received Jesus and been given the right to become one of God's family. He'd never thought of it like that before; he'd never really thought of it at all. Now he saw how important it was. He wished Jeff had been here this morning.

The thing was—British or Brazilian. One of God's children or——

Ross decided there and then.

CHAPTER EIGHTEEN

THE CARTOON

Ross placed the Bible on his table, and opened it at the Gospel of John. There was one good thing about that verse: if he did forget where it came, then it wouldn't take very long to go through from the beginning until he found it. He looked at the title of the chapter, 'The Coming of Christ', then tried going through slowly until he hit on the part he wanted. Some of it was hard to understand—not the bit they had this morning; he got hold of that easily: 'To all who did receive Jesus, he gave the right to become children of God.' Then, leaving the new Bible open on the table, Ross went downstairs to dinner.

Mr. Rich was dozing in the armchair, while outside on the concrete path that ran by the house Peter was cleaning his bike. Carol moved around the room aimlessly, then looked out at Peter, aware that he wished to be on his own. Ross was thinking of Jeff. Jeff ought to be all right by the Easter holidays, and that left the one week on his own at school and then three weeks' freedom together. He watched the pale sunlight on the faded carpet, the frayed blue edge, and his mind was back with the evidence at the bakery, the stars and stripes which he had done nothing about yet. He went upstairs and, getting onto the bed, stared out at the lime tree and the building site. Immediately beneath the window Peter was tinkering with his bike. Ross opened the window cautiously and looked down at the top of his brother's head, watching the blustery wind playing with his mop of hair. At length he withdrew into his room, and was about to close the window, when he caught sight of a policeman's helmet above the front hedge, progressing surely and certainly towards their house. He listened. The gate whined; it clicked shut. Ross glanced down once more at Peter—Peter, no longer concentrating on his bike, Peter standing with his greasy hands together. Then the door-bell pealed through the house.

Ross closed the window, his heart pounding. Something told him there was more trouble to come, a lot more trouble. Towards Peter he now felt a sudden sympathy. Leaving his room, he descended the first half flight of stairs. The front door was open and there was no mistaking that voice that come from the hall beneath.

"Ah, good afternoon, Mrs. Rich. Sorry to bother you once again."

Ross crept down the stairs, and on the landing below met Carol. They looked at each other silently, while Mrs. Rich conducted the policeman into the room at the back. She must have heard them on the stairs, for she called to Carol to go and fetch Peter.

"Oh dear," sighed Carol, "I wish Pete would ———" Ross followed her into the hall, and then stood waiting while she went out into the garden. He wondered what she was saying to Peter. The next moment they both came in through the back door and, without so much as a glance at Ross, Peter went straight in to meet the policeman. Ross and Carol hovered outside the door, not feeling it right to intrude too openly on Peter's trouble, yet unable to walk away and leave him alone.

"Interrupted your work, I see," began the policeman. "Well, I won't keep you long."

Peter had moved across the room out of his vision, but Ross could see the policeman, standing with his back to the window, unrolling a paper. "I wonder if you could identify this. The paper was purchased at Flemings, and the lettering is similar to some done by members of the Art Group at Simms School, though the style of the illustration is individual, to say the least."

Ross gazed at the daring cartoon of a slave owner, done in red and black, and the word 'Justice' in bold letters followed by a large question mark. He wasn't sure what it was all about, but of one thing he was quite sure—it was Peter's work. Now, all too plainly, he saw something else—the purpose behind that question of the policeman, "Any others in your family good at drawing?" and his easy answer, "Carol can't draw for nuts, but Peter's pretty good. He's going to be an architect." He felt Carol's eyes on him, he felt her accusation, 'You again; you've got him into trouble again. You're a rotten tell-tale.' And from far away he heard the policeman's voice, "I see you do recognise the work", and Peter's curt answer, "It's mine."

"I see." With those words it seemed as though Peter was doomed. "And you managed to exhibit this inside the foreman's office, next door."

There was no reply from Peter.

"To achieve this, you entered the premises on the night of Tuesday."

"I went onto the building site on Tuesday night."

"A pity you couldn't have admitted this before. So you broke the office window to gain an entry and——"

"I stole nothing."

"But, Peter, why did you do it?" pleaded Mrs. Rich.

"And what were you protesting about this time?" Mr. Rich added.

"Does it matter?"

"Yes, Peter, it does matter very much. The thing is, what had it to do with you?"

"Of course it had to do with me, with everyone."

"And who, might I ask, informed you of the little bit of bother next door?" queried the policeman. But Peter kept silent.

It was then Mrs. Rich became aware of the two eavesdroppers, and for Peter's sake came across and closed the door.

"Why doesn't he say something about that lorry?" Ross was agitated for Peter, worried by the answers he avoided giving.

"What would that prove?" said Carol. "I don't know why he had to stick that thing in the office. I suppose it was so jolly good he had to go and— Oh, Ross, we've got to do something."

CHAPTER NINETEEN

ALLEGIANCE

Ross stared miserably at the closed door. Do something? What could they do? All he wanted to do was to get away from Carol's meaning 'You got Pete in this mess', away from the questioning that was being pursued behind that dark door, away from the final verdict of Peter in court, Peter shutting himself up in his room. The newness of the morning's experience, of finding that verse and knowing it was meant for him was robbed of its first excitement. And yet it couldn't mean that he didn't belong to God any more.

Without waiting to put on his coat, Ross ran out of the house into Lewis Road, past the now silent building site, into the High Street. There were only two people to whom he wanted to go—Jeff and Mr. Wilson. And they wouldn't let him see Jeff.

The High Street was deserted, the shops shuttered, and yet it drew him. He went slowly towards the bakery, his mind in a turmoil. The word over which he had stumbled in the reading came back to him—allegiance. Up to now he'd been concerned about sticking by Jeff—and there couldn't be anything wrong with that, because Jeff was his friend. But sticking by Jeff had meant that

G

he was unable to help Peter. So what was he to do? It had to be one or the other. Now it didn't seem the same; now it was being loyal to Jesus. The thing was, he wasn't sure how it was going to work out, and a little fear stabbed him, lest in giving his allegiance to Jesus he should bring trouble on Jeff.

Ross turned round and retraced his steps, making for Wicket Lane. By the time he reached the Old Barn he was red-faced with hurrying. Everything here was the same—the five-bar gate pushed back and propped up by the wall, the sunlight on the tall, weedy-looking grass about the trees. He made straight for the out-house, the 'bird ringing station' as Mr. Wilson called it. The door was closed so Ross peered in through the window, but there was no sign of Alexander Wilson. The conservatory, too, was empty, and in the stretch of ground ahead there was no sign of anyone. With a sinking feeling of failure, he approached the back door of the house and rapped timidly, but there was no response. He tried again, but still there was no answer to his knocking. For a moment Ross sensed despair. How could he decide what to do? And he had come all this way for nothing. He was angry with Mr. Wilson for not being there to help him. How was he to know the right thing to do? 'I think God always lets us know—in time.' That was what Mr. Wilson had said. Ross wanted to know now.

He made his way back to Simms Wood and wandered between the trees. Still round the base of the beech trees were the shrivelled remains of last year's nuts. Sort of evidence—like the flag. If only he was clever enough to work things out! But he wasn't.

The thing was, God knew; He must know, because He was God.

He sat down on an old tree stump. It was chilly between the trees, and now he missed the protection of his raincoat. Only a few days ago he and Jeff had been excited about solving the mystery of the building site, hopefully listing all the evidence, even when they knew there was little chance of finding the solution. Now all the fever of finding out who did it was overshadowed by the irksome responsibility of deciding what to do. It was all Peter's fault; he shouldn't have been on the building site. If it wasn't for Peter, then he wouldn't be so worried.

"Dear God," he prayed, "please tell me what to do." Then Ross knew he didn't want to have to do anything; he just wanted things to be straightened out, without too much trouble, without too much trouble to himself. "Dear God", he began once more, "I'm sorry about things being all wrong. If you tell me what to do you'd better help me do it as well. Amen."

He decided to go and ask how Jeff was, and then go home. The wind blew between the trees, and Ross shivered as he began to hurry to the High Street. Turning down by the side of the Sampsons' shop, he could hear voices in the yard. He didn't really want to meet Mr. Sampson. If he could knock at the back door, Jeff might come to the top of the wooden stairs that rose steeply in front of the door, and they could talk. Ross approached quietly.

Mr. Sampson was talking with another man, and both of them were considering the bake-house at

the end of the yard. Across the yard, between Ross
and the two men, was an open lorry, which was
either about to be backed into the open garage with
which it was lined up, or had just been taken out.
Ross's heart raced. Brown paint—but then lots of
trucks had brown paint. All the same, it was brown.
What ought he to do? He'd asked God to help, and
here he was with the chance of discovering something. It was just waiting for him. Mr. Sampson
and his companion had their backs to him, as Ross,
drawn by the chance of seeing that flag once more,
crept between the lorry and the shop premises to
the open garage. Inside the garage it was darker.
On the left was Sampson's delivery van, its cream
paint showing up in the darkness. Ross crept
further in, glancing from the dim corners to the
old rafters overhead. He faced outwards again, and
directly in his line of vision was the back of the
lorry, tailboard down, some sacking heaped against
the cab. If he went down he could see the number
plate of the lorry—that was one thing he must get.
Before he stooped he saw the tell-tale stars and
stripes at the rear of the garage, half obscured by
the delivery van. No longer concerned with the
number plate, he laid hold of the evidence, a soiled
and dusty emblem of the United States.

Now he could hear the two men more distinctly.

"Thank you, Mr. Sampson; a few more weeks'll
see me right."

"That's all right, Mr. Jenkins; but I don't
reckon to have you use the garage on Sundays, all
the same."

Clutching the flag, Ross was now concerned to

get a view of Mr. Jenkins. From the dark recess of the garage he watched him get into the cab and start up the engine. Dark hair, not very much of it, reddish face, tall and——

Deftly and accurately Mr. Jenkins backed his lorry into the waiting garage, closed and fastened the garage doors. He nodded to Mr. Sampson and went out into the High Street.

CHAPTER TWENTY

LATE AGAIN

Peter was standing by his window, looking out onto the front garden, still stunned by the events of the afternoon. He hadn't thought it would come to this.

"Pete." Carol pushed the door open.

"Yeh." Peter still had his back to her, not wanting nor intending to explain what had happened.

"It's Ross."

Peter turned round sharply and saw Carol's scared face. "Ross?"

"He isn't home."

Peter shrugged his shoulders. "So what! You know what Ross and Jeff are. Anyway, why ask me?"

"But Pete, Jeff's got German measles, so he can't be with Jeff, and it's ten past five."

"Who says he can't be with Jeff? You bet that's where he is. He'll turn up." Peter leant against the wall; his own problems were far more pressing than his young brother being late for tea.

Carol, still anxious, remained by the door, recalling the strange expression in Ross's eyes just before, coat-less and cap-less he had bolted out of the front door. Peter and Ross—what horrible secrets were they hiding between them, and why was one afraid of the other, each trying to conceal his actions from the other? "But Pete, he just dashed out without his coat—when the policeman was here."

Peter pushed past and leapt up the stairs to the attic, followed by Carol. They went up to Ross's table, and, surprised, looked down at the open Bible.

"Of all the cheek! That's mine," complained Carol. Peter hardly heard her; his eyes were scanning the two pages spread before him. 'The light shines on in the dark, and the darkness has never mastered it.' Why did that startle him? Why was it so real? He shifted his eyes to the right-hand page, till his attention was drawn to the very words that Ross had been considering: 'To all who did receive him, to those who have yielded him their allegiance, he gave the right to become children of God.' Once he had thought about it, but that was a year ago, and he had pushed it from his mind.

He walked across to the window and surveyed the dark trees of Simms Wood. Of course nothing was up with Ross; if he wasn't at Jeff's he was probably climbing trees in Simms Wood. Suppose the silly kid had had another crack like last week?

"Pete, suppose something's——" Carol was wondering why the Bible was there on the table, and what it had to do with Ross's lateness.

"Don't panic, girl." He turned back to the open Bible. Ross knew something, but how much?

"We've been a bit rotten to him," admitted Carol sheepishly, her conscience disturbed, "even if he did mess things up for you. What's going to happen to you, Pete?" She had been reluctant to question him up to now.

"Oh, first offender," he tried to appear casual; "juvenile court.' He slumped onto Ross's bed. "It's all so crazy—useless."

"Carol!"

"That's Mum," said Carol.

They ran downstairs.

"Have you seen Ross?"

"He went out, when——"

"But that's three hours ago, Carol, and he knows tea's at five on Sundays. Did he say——" Mrs. Rich saw the doubt in their eyes, the doubt that was invading her mind. What was Ross up to now? And he'd seemed so different. What could be bothering him, when this morning he was on top of the world?

"Trust Ross to be late," said Peter.

"It's not just that. It's the something that you and Ross——"

"I'll go round to Jeff's," interrupted Peter; "he might be there."

By the time he returned with the information that Ross had not been seen at the bakery, it was gone half past five.

"Ross wants a good shaking up," said Mr. Rich severely. "Time he learnt he can't come and go as he pleases. We'll have tea; it isn't as though it's the first time he's kept us waiting."

But tea was a cheerless meal, each of them listening for Ross's footsteps.

"What about this place where he went the other day—the chap who does the bird-ringing," suggested Mr. Rich, now as anxious as the others. "I believe I can actually remember where it is."

"The Old Barn, Wicket Lane. So can I," added Peter. "I'll go round on my bike." For more reasons than one he was anxious to reach Ross first.

"No, I'll take the car; that way we'll get him home sooner."

"Perhaps he's on the phone." Mrs. Rich got up from the table.

"Now, I don't remember the man's name."

"It was Wilson," she added.

"Well, by the time we've got through the list in the directory, I'll be halfway there."

"I'm going, too," announced Peter.

"As you wish," conceded Mr. Rich, still put out with Peter for his stubborn refusal to co-operate with the police.

"It's six o'clock," said Carol lamely, wishing she too could go in search of Ross.

CHAPTER TWENTY-ONE

THE SEARCH

The car bumped on the ruts in Wicket Lane.

"Must be this one." Peter peered through the windscreen to see if there was anything to indicate the name or number of the house.

"Since it's not any of the others, it must be," decided Mr. Rich, drawing up outside the Old Barn. "You can go in, if you like, and ask about Ross. We don't want to alarm Mr. Wilson by a solemn deputation of two of the family. Call me if you want me."

Wondering what had prompted his father's offer, Peter slammed the car door and hurried into the Old Barn. The sky was overcast, and there was none of that brightness about the place which appealed to Ross. To Peter it was dreary and uncared for. Mr. Wilson, who was scattering crumbs to the birds, turned at the sound of approaching footsteps, and inspected Peter over the top of his spectacles.

"Mr. Wilson?" asked Peter.

"That's it; Mr. Wilson." He smiled at Peter's awkwardness.

"Has Ross—he's my brother—has he been round here this afternoon?"

A puzzled expression came into Mr. Wilson's eyes. "Ross is your brother, yes, I can see he is like you. Has he sent you to see me?"

Peter grew impatient. Mr. Wilson was carrying on as though there was all the time in the world. "No, I just want to know if he's been here at all."

"Ross has not been here today. I was not expecting him this afternoon, but I have been out, so it is possible he may have called and no one was here. Still, he was here twice yesterday. And you are Peter. And something is the matter, yes? With Ross?"

"No, not exactly; just that he went out about two o'clock and we don't know where he is. Mum was getting worried, and Dad thought he might have come round here." Peter tried to make out that he himself was not perturbed at Ross's non-appearance.

"And you are worried, too—about Ross? And about yourself?"

Peter grew angry at the thought that Ross might have been blabbing about his affairs.

"You do not have to tell me anything," continued Mr. Wilson quietly, "but I, too, am a little worried about Ross."

"Oh."

"And you do not know where else to look, because you will have enquired at Jeff's already. Is that it?"

"Yes."

"Tell me, Peter, did Ross say anything to you yesterday evening, or this morning perhaps?"

"What d'you mean? I don't understand."

"Ross has told me about the trouble. Did he mention something new about the building site, after he left here yesterday afternoon?"

"No, nothing. Only, well—perhaps he did mean to tell me something, but I was fed up with him over several things, and I shut him up. Then," Peter hesitated, "then this afternoon the police came."

"The police came?" Mr. Wilson stood deep in thought. "To see you, Peter?"

"Yes; there was a drawing of mine, a cartoon, and they found it in the foreman's office."

"They found it." Mr. Wilson's eyes twinkled, "But you would not dream of saying how it got there?"

Peter laughed. He was beginning to like this character with the foreign accent.

"And Ross was there when the policeman called, and he heard what was said?"

"Some of it. He was there at the beginning; then my sister said he bunked. That was at two o'clock."

"Something alarmed him. Now what would have alarmed him? Can you think what it was?"

"I suppose thinking I might have to—well, Ross might have thought anything. After all, he's only a kid."

"Maybe he is, but perhaps there is one thing he might want to do—to help you."

"To help me?"

"Yes, I think he might want to check on a piece of evidence. I don't know. I think Ross will do what is right. I am sure he will ask God to make it quite clear to him. And there is one thing quite clear to me : we have to go to Sampson's bakery."

"I've been there already."

"All the same, I am quite sure it is there we must go.' Mr. Wilson gave a decisive nod to his head. "Quite sure. When I saw Ross sitting there in church this morning, I felt concerned about him. I thought soon there will be a great deal of trouble about this affair at the building site, and Ross will need someone to help and guide him. So I prayed for him, and for you, Peter, because you are in trouble, too. No, I am not asking any questions. Now I will tell my Teresa that I am going out again for a while."

"My father's got the car outside."

"Splendid. I will be back."

Peter watched him go through the kitchen door. Ross had shared something with Mr. Wilson; perhaps it all had something to do with the Bible on Ross's table. And Ross would have told him, if he hadn't snubbed him.

CHAPTER TWENTY-TWO

SAMPSON'S BAKERY

Parking the car outside the shop, the three hurried into the yard at the rear. Mr. Wilson looked round, sensing the atmosphere of the place.

"So this is Jeff's home." Then he stood contemplating the ill-fitting garage doors, while Mr. Rich knocked on the back door. Peter heard steps descending the wooden stairs, as he had done earlier.

Mrs. Sampson opened the door, and was taken aback at seeing Peter again, Peter accompanied by his father and another man. She had dark hair like Jeff, and was short and plump.

"Good afternoon, or evening, Mrs. Sampson," began Mr. Rich, then noticed Mr. Sampson coming down the stairs to join them. "Sorry to bother you both on a Sunday afternoon, but Ross hasn't turned up."

"Oh dear, these boys!" Mrs. Sampson leant towards her visitors, "Don't let Jeff hear; he'll be in such a state."

"He's already in a state," said Mr. Sampson. "It's no good trying to kid Jeff that Ross will have arrived by now."

"This is Mr. Wilson; he's a friend of Ross and Jeff." Mr. Rich made the introduction.

"Yes, they are my friends. Are you quite sure

Ross hasn't been here this afternoon. I know you haven't seen him, but is there anyone else might have seen him?"

"No one comes here on a Sunday afternoon," Mrs. Sampson assured him.

"Well, as it happens, Dave Jenkins was around. He took the truck out about one o'clock. I came down when I heard him bringing it back into the yard——"

"Mr. Jenkins?" asked Mr. Wilson.

"Yes, he's been using the spare garage for a few weeks, and he did some sort of a job this afternoon; but I told him I wasn't counting on him using the garage on Sundays. I didn't let him have it on those conditions; after all, this is our home."

"So Mr. Jenkins was here, and you came down to have a word with him; what time was that?"

"About four-thirty—bit earlier, maybe."

"And while Mr. Jenkins was out with his lorry, did he leave the garage open?"

"No."

"But when he returned he drove the truck into the yard."

"Always backs it—it's no joke trying to turn a truck in this yard. All right with the little van."

"He backed it, opened the garage door, and then you turned up."

"That's it."

"And then?"

"Well, we chatted for a bit. I didn't want to appear unreasonable, so we talked over one or two things. I showed him the guttering along the bakehouse. He's a builder, on his own in business, so

I asked his opinion; then I made it clear to him about Sundays."

"Well, if I could have a look in the garage, it would settle things. May I, Mr. Sampson?" requested Mr. Wilson.

They were all curious what it was behind those locked doors could possibly settle things, and at the same time they were annoyed with Mr. Wilson, irritated with him for keeping them guessing.

"We can get into Dave Jenkins' part through the right-hand garage—it's all one garage, really—used to be the old stables. If you get in one, you get in the lot."

"I'll fetch the keys." Mr. Sampson went indoors, and they could hear Jeff's voice. "Where's Ross, Dad? Where is he?" Absorbed by the task of gaining an entry to the garage, they failed to notice Jeff in a navy jersey and jeans standing by the back entrance.

Mr. Sampson pulled back the rickety wooden door. "There you are, Mr. Wilson; it's all yours." He was curt, feeling he had been ordered around.

Mr. Wilson made his way by the side of the baker's van; on his left was the open truck, half shrouded in darkness. Was it the very truck Ross had seen on the building site? And had Ross seen it here? He moved slowly between the two vehicles.

"It is almost too dark to see." His voice sounded strange from the depths of the garage, and the waiting party, unable to follow him, since by so doing they would block the passage of light, were tense and impatient. "Ross!"

From the back door, even Jeff heard Mr. Wilson's muffled exclamation, and ran out into the yard. "Ross. I got to see Ross. Rossy, it's me—Jeff."

"Ross!" Peter exclaimed. He would have given anything to be there beside him. Instead, he seized hold of Jeff. "He'll be O.K., Jeff. Hang on a bit."

Mrs. Sampson, too, tried to quieten Jeff, but, mystified by Ross's presence in the garage, he refused to be comforted, for no sound of Ross's familiar voice came from the darkness of the garage.

Mr. Rich moved in to find Ross, while Mr. Sampson got into the delivery van ready to drive it out of the garage. "Can I shift her? Is it safe?" he called.

"Get her out," answered Mr. Rich.

The moments seemed hours as Mr. Sampson first fumbled for the ignition key, then started up the engine. Slowly he drove the van out into the yard. Mrs. Sampson tried to shield Jeff; and Peter, too, held to him firmly. It was the least he could do for Ross. He saw his father and Mr. Wilson bending over by the rear of the open truck. Mr. Sampson, getting out of the van, came across to the garage.

"It's the truck'll need shifting."

Mr. Rich stood up. "Get the doctor and don't make any attempt to shift this lorry without him." In that moment Peter caught sight of Ross, his leg apparently trapped beneath the rear wheel, and clutched across his chest—a tattered Stars and Stripes.

H

CHAPTER TWENTY-THREE

TRAPPED

"I'll ring for the ambulance. Jeff, you come with me." Mrs. Sampson had no intention of leaving Jeff in the yard to see how badly Ross was hurt.

"Give Jenkins a ring. Tell him we'll need him to jack up his lorry," called Mr. Sampson from the garage.

"And I'll let Ross's mum know he's safe, Mr. Rich. Don't you worry about that," assured Mrs. Sampson.

Mr. Rich had not moved from Ross's side, and now Mr. Sampson got beneath the truck.

"Wheel's not right over that leg. Back of the truck must have caught him and pitched him down. Can't think what he wanted to get in there for. He'll have got a nasty crack on the head on these old cobbles. That's what's knocked him out. I'll get that other door open; then we can see a bit better. Spare key's here somewhere or other."

Mr. Wilson left Ross's side and drew Peter into the yard. "Peter," he said quietly, "there is something you can do to help."

"Of course; I'll do anything."

"Then you will go now, straight away, and fetch the police."

"The police?" That was the last thing Peter

wanted; he had had quite enough for one day. "How will that help Ross?" he objected.

"It is very important the police should be here when Ross is released, and it looks as though Mr. Jenkins will be here as well. Ross was trying to do something to help you, Peter, of that I am sure, and I don't want it to be wasted."

"O.K. I'll go."

"Say your brother is trapped beneath a lorry. You know, I think they will come at once for one of the Rich family."

Peter shot along the High Street to the police station, all the time eager to be back at Sampson's yard with Ross. It was the first time he had been in the red brick station, though he had known it all his life—the narrow strip of garden in front, the old-fashioned lamp with blue glass. Inside, it was so ordinary: an enquiry window by the door, and, on the walls of the office ahead, an assortment of posters and printed notices. Peter knew it was more than likely that his policeman would still be on duty; and there he was, only without his helmet he looked younger and more approachable.

"Ah, changed your mind, have you?" he asked.

"It's nothing to do with that. It's Ross, my brother; he's trapped under a lorry at the bakery— Sampson's shop."

"Well, I'll be blowed! You don't stay out of trouble for long in your family, do you? If you wait a moment while I give some instructions, I'll come along with you."

Meanwhile at the bakery the sing-song note of the ambulance was heard, and, at the same time as the ambulance men came into the yard, a worried and breathless Mr. Jenkins arrived on the scene. Mrs. Sampson was making it plain to Jeff that if he didn't stay in the doorway he'd have to go back upstairs. After all, he still had German measles, even if he did feel quite well.

Then the ambulance men were crouching beside Ross, sizing up the difficulties of getting him out.

"Better not risk it—get the man to jack it up," decided one.

"Why not release the brake and get a couple of them to ease her forward. Leg's not trapped; just the rear of the tyre pressing against it. Near thing, though. Bit of luck it stopped just when it did."

Mr. Jenkins began to talk excitedly. "Look, I never saw the kid. Mr. Sampson was here when I backed the lorry; he'll tell you."

"Never mind that; take the brake off when I say."

Mr. Jenkins got into the cab, while Mr. Rich and Mr. Sampson stationed themselves at the rear of the truck.

"Now," came the order.

Slowly they eased the truck away from Ross's inert form. Mr. Jenkins alighted and, turning to see the plight of the boy who had been knocked down by his vehicle, failed to see Peter and the policeman enter the yard. Freed from the over-shadowing truck, Ross could now be seen lying on the uneven cobbles. His right hand with which he must have picked up the flag was flung out at his side by the force of his fall, dragging the Stars and Stripes across his body, while the other arm was limp by his side. He looked small and lost in the comfortless garage.

Mr. Wilson tapped Mr. Jenkins on the arm. "Seems he wants to take something of yours with him."

Mr. Jenkins, obviously agitated by the fact that his truck had been involved in the accident, made no answer.

"Any particular interest to you—the Stars and Stripes, I mean?" pursued Mr. Wilson as they watched the stretcher being placed in readiness.

"No. Matter of fact, it was in a load of rags I got. Used it sometimes for tying on timber or scaffolding, that sort of thing. Kind of took my fancy."

"I understand that. Not the sort of thing anyone else has waving at the end of a load. Wouldn't be anyone else on the Lewis Road building site on the morning of Tuesday last week with a Stars and Stripes tied on their load?"

They were lifting Ross onto the stretcher as Mrs. Rich hurried into the yard followed by Carol, and in the commotion Mr. Jenkins was unaware that the policeman was standing behind him.

"So the Stars and Stripes belongs to you, Mr. Jenkins?"

He turned and saw the questioner.

"You're a builder. Wouldn't be difficult to place three dozen sets of chrome bath fittings, or a case of chrome door handles? How did you know there was a strike on, when it would be easy work picking up those goods? And, come to that, how did you know they had been delivered the day before?"

The blankets were wrapped round Ross. They

were moving out of the yard with the stretcher, but Ross's face was not so pale as that of Mr. Jenkins. The builder watched the procession. It was not the boy who was trapped; it was him, trapped by a bit of a thing like that Stars and Stripes that took his fancy.

Peter watched them put Ross in the ambulance, his mother and father crowd in after, and then the ambulance start on its way to Weststorth Hospital.

"Well, Peter?"

He turned to see that Mr. Wilson, too, was watching the disappearing ambulance.

"Perhaps we can hear your part of the story some time, eh, Peter?"

"There's not very much to tell."

But Carol was eager to hear, for, between the two of them, Peter and Ross had kept her guessing for a long time. "Go on, Pete."

"We had a sixth form debate that evening. It was about industrial disputes and workers' rights; and one of the boys whose father has been working on the Lewis Road site told us what had been going on there, and that there was going to be a strike, a day's strike on the Tuesday, as a protest. We felt pretty strongly about it so we thought it would be a good idea if we did something about it, too; stuck some posters around. I sketched out that one that got me into trouble. It seemed such a marvellous idea when we planned it; we never thought about trespassing, or really finding out what had happened. The only chance we had of getting our posters displayed was to put them up while no one was around to stop us, and we were tickled to bits about them wondering who had put them up. So we decided to put them up that night. They'd all been dead keen about it, but when it came to doing it there weren't any offers. I felt shamed after all the talk, because I wasn't all that keen, either. Anyway, I said I'd go if one of them would come with me."

"Who was that?" asked Carol.

"Not who you'd think. Alan Povey. It was me made him, and now he's dead scared lest his aunt and uncle hear about it. It's rotten luck on him; he'd never have done it if it wasn't for me going on at him. I said I was going to put my cartoon in the foreman's office. It was locked; and when I tried the window, the whole thing came right out and smashed. Alan was petrified, and then when I told him about the police and the theft, that was the last straw. Funny about Ross hearing that noise."

"You know, Peter, your friend Alan is always going to be afraid, until——"

"But he couldn't tell them; they wouldn't understand we didn't mean any harm." Peter interrupted Mr. Wilson.

"All the same, he will always be afraid. It is like that with us and God, until we are open and honest. We are afraid, so we pretend we have done nothing, or else we pretend God isn't there. And there is no need to be afraid, since He sent Jesus to take all our punishment, so that we could go free. If Alan understood that, he would feel differently. Otherwise he will have to live with his fear, and fear is not a very nice companion."

Peter was silent. He knew how scared he had

been, and how impossible it had been to shake off
the fear that pursued him.

"I suppose I shouldn't have goaded him on."

They were interrupted by the policeman coming out of Sampson's yard accompanied by Mr.
Jenkins.

"Goodnight, Mr. Wilson; goodnight, Peter. I'll
be having another chat with you about the little
matter we were discussing this afternoon."

"Goodnight," said Peter.

The three of them lingered, watching the retreat-
ing figures, thinking of Ross, and wondering if he
was going to be all right.

CHAPTER TWENTY-FOUR

31265 AGAIN

"Hullo, Mr. Wilson." Ross looked round the ward as he proudly held the receiver. "31265 speaking. This is a private telephone call from the hospital."

"Very exciting. I feel very important, too, having a call from 31265R for Ross. How are you this morning?"

"I'm O.K. I think I'm coming home tomorrow."

"Fine."

"Mr. Wilson, you were super, catching Mr. Jenkins."

"Well, you weren't so bad yourself."

"I was going to write and thank you for finding me, but my arm still hurts, so Dad said he'd fix a phone call for me. It's much better than a letter."

"A letter would have been good, but not everyone can have a telephone call from hospital, so perhaps this is best."

"I was going to tell you about the man we had on Sunday. He told us some jolly interesting things about Brazil, and if you want to be a Brazilian you can't be British as well. You have to choose."

"Is that so?"

Ross watched the nurse down the ward, and another nurse come through the swing doors. He whispered into the mouthpiece, "The nurse with the list is coming; she asks you what you'd like for dinner. I don't want to miss her or I might not get ice cream."

"No. I don't think I would want to miss her, either."

"It's all right; she's doing the other side first."

"So we don't have to worry about your dinner yet."

"That man on Sunday asked me to read. It was from John, but I can't remember which verse, but I'd know when I got to it."

"About receiving Jesus, and then being made one of God's family."

"How did you know?"

"So you did that, Ross."

"I reckon I did, Mr. Wilson."

"That is the best thing you have ever done."

"Then it had a bit about allegiance; that's what made me go to Jeff's Sunday afternoon. Before, I couldn't make up my mind which one I ought to stand up for—Jeff or Pete. Then I was sure about going to the bakery."

"Jeff and I have got it planned for you both to come to Wicket Lane."

"Jeff? Wish I could see Jeff."

"You will soon. Perhaps you can help ring one of the birds. I will show you how to hold them while it is done."

The whiteness of the ward dimmed; its bustle and activity seemed far away. Instead, Ross could feel the warmth and the freedom of the Old Barn, the long grass, the trees in the little orchard. Hospital had had its excitement, especially the presents

—a book called *Birds of the night* from Mr. Wilson, a new Bible of his own from Mum and Dad, and a set of felt pencils from Carol and Peter.

"Mr. Wilson, what's the number of the next ring?"

"That's my secret."

"You know, if that blackbird hadn't died, I'd never have known about you, Mr. Wilson."

"No, Ross, that's quite true. But just think, if Jesus hadn't died on the cross for us, and risen again, we'd never know God."

"I think the nurse is coming. I expect she'll say I've had long enough."

"Well, goodbye, 31265. The ringing station will be ready for you as soon as you are well."

"Goodbye, Mr. Wilson. Say, could the next number be Jeff's?"